MORE PRAISE FOR

"The power is in the writing. Mr. Meno is a superb
—Hubert Selby, Jr.

for *Hairstyles of the Damned*

A selection of the Barnes & Noble Discover Great New Writers Program

"Captures both the sweetness and sting of adolescence with unflinching honesty."
—*Entertainment Weekly*

"Joe Meno writes with the energy, honesty, and emotional impact of the best punk rock. From the opening sentence to the very last word, *Hairstyles of the Damned* held me in his grip."
—Jim DeRogatis, pop music critic, *Chicago Sun-Times*

"The most authentic young voice since J.D. Salinger's Holden Caulfield . . . A darn good book."
—*Daily Southtown*

"Sensitive, well-observed, often laugh-out-loud funny . . . You won't regret a moment of the journey."
—*Chicago Tribune*

"Meno gives his proverbial coming-of-age tale a punk-rock edge, as seventeen-year-old Chicagoan Brian Oswald tries to land his first girlfriend . . . Meno ably explores Brian's emotional uncertainty and his poignant youthful search for meaning . . . His gabby, heartfelt, and utterly believable take on adolescence strikes a winning chord."
—*Publishers Weekly*

"Meno is a romantic at heart. Not the greeting card kind, or the Harlequin paperback version, but the type who thinks, deep down, that things matter, that art can change lives."
—*Elgin Courier News*

"Funny and charming and sad and real. The adults are sparingly yet poignantly drawn, especially the fathers, who slip through without saying much but make a profound impression."
—*Chicago Journal*

"A funny, hard-rocking first-person tale of teenage angst and discovery."
—*Booklist*

"Underneath his angst, Brian, the narrator of *Hairstyles of the Damned,* possesses a disarming sense of compassion which allows him to worm his way into the reader's heart. It is this simple contradiction that makes Meno's portrait of adolescence so convincing: He has dug up and displayed for us the secret paradox of the teenage years, the desire to belong pitted against the need for individuality—a constant clash of hate and love."

—NewPages.com

"Joe Meno knows Chicago's south side the way Jane Goodall knew chimps and apes—which is to say, he really knows it. He also knows about the early '90s, punk rock, and awkward adolescence. Best of all, he knows the value of entertainment. *Hairstyles of the Damned* is proof positive."

—John McNally, author of *The Book of Ralph*

"Filled with references to dozens of bands and mix-tape set lists, the book's heart and soul is driven by a teenager's life-changing discovery of punk's social and political message . . . Meno's alter ego, Brian Oswald, is a modern-day Holden Caulfield . . . It's a funny, sweet, and, at times, hard-hitting story with a punk vibe."

—Mary Houlihan, *Chicago Sun-Times*

"Meno's language is rhythmic and honest, expressing things proper English never could. And you've got to hand it to the author, who pulled off a very good trick: The book *is* punk rock. It's not just *about* punk rock; it embodies the idea of punk—it's pissed off at authority, it won't groom itself properly, and it irritates. Yet its rebellious spirit is inspiring and right on the mark."

—*SF Weekly*

"This book is hella good. Joe Meno manages to sink into the teenage-outcast experience, challenge segregation, and provide step-by-step instructions on dyeing hair pink in this realistic account of finding your identity. After reading *Hairstyles of the Damned*, I'm glad I'm not in high school anymore."

—Amy Schroeder, *Venus* magazine

"*Hairstyles of the Damned* is observational comedy of the best kind, each glittering small detail offering up a wave of memories for anyone alive in the latter part of the previous century. Did you imagine you had forgotten the smell of arcades, the allure of muscle cars, the dress codes and emotional rebellions, the cringing horror of adolescence? Beware: Joe Meno can make you remember."

—HipMama.com

"What makes *Hairstyles of the Damned* compelling is Meno's ability to create the rhythm of teen-speak without pandering, and his ability to infuse the story with pop-culture references. A good read for those wanting to remember their youthful mischief."

—*Tablet*

"Meno's recounting of first concerts, first loves, and the first tragedies of adolescence are awesomely paired with the heavy backbeat of late-'80s subculture. The contagious foot tapping that is symptomatic of a good record is the same energy that drives you as you follow Meno's narrative."

—FresnoFamous.com

for *The Boy Detective Fails*

"This is postmodern fiction with a head *and* a heart, addressing such depressing issues as suicide, death, loneliness, failure, anomie, and guilt with compassion, humor, and even whimsy. Meno's best work yet; highly recommended."

—*Library Journal* (starred review)

"Comedic, imaginative, empathic, atmospheric, archetypal, and surpassingly sweet, Meno's finely calibrated fantasy investigates the precincts of grief, our longing to combat chaos with reason, and the menace and magic concealed within everyday life."

—*Booklist* (starred review)

"Mood is everything here, and Meno tunes it like a master . . . a full-tilt collision of wish-fulfillment and unrequited desires that's thrilling, yet almost unbearably sad."

—*Kirkus Reviews* (starred review)

"A delicate blend of whimsy and edginess. Meno packs his novel with delightful subtext."

—*Entertainment Weekly*

"A radiantly creative masterpiece . . . Meno's imaginative genius spins heartache into hope within this fanciful growing-up tale that glows like no other."

—PopMatters.com

"The search for truth, love, and redemption is surprising and absorbing. Swaddled in melancholy and gentle humor, it builds in power as the clues pile up."

—*Publishers Weekly*

"An easy to read sometimes dark tale with a perfect ending. On a scale of 1 to 5, I give it a 4.8."

—*Futures Mystery Anthology Magazine*

"At the bottom of this Pandora's box of mirthful absurdity, there's heartbreak and longing, eerie beauty and hope."

—*Philadelphia Weekly*

"Verbally delectable."

—*Chicago Tribune*

"Marinated in mood, richly crafted and devoid of irony, Meno's newest novel is imbued with both the hopeful and the romantic."

—*Time Out Chicago*

"Moving, elegant prose."

—*Washington Post Express*

"Surreal, mysterious, and dreamlike."

—*NewCity Chicago*

"You know that friend of yours who keeps trying to get you to read his half written novel about his quarter-life crisis? Do yourself a favor and read Joe Meno's version of turning thirty instead."

—*The L Magazine*

"It's *Encyclopedia Brown* without the milk and cookies."

—*Chicago Sun-Times*

for *How the Hula Girl Sings*

"An intimate book, wrapped up in the bent logic and lame emotional politics of folks tied by memory and old-school loathings . . . The novel succeeds because Meno gives Luce Lemay the struggling soul of a poet looking to bend anguish into possibility . . . offering what Raymond Carver used to call 'glimpses' of what else might be, flashes of another, more comforting brand of reality."

—*NewCity Chicago*

"Meno's poetic and visceral style perfectly captures the seedy locale, and he finds the sadness behind violence and the anger behind revenge. Fans of hard-boiled pulp fiction will particularly enjoy this novel."

—*Booklist*

"For such grim subject matter, the author moves the story along at a surprisingly fast and easy pace, never succumbing to the overkill that American gothic tales are often prone to, seeming to take his inspiration equally from the stories of Jim Thompson and the lyrics of Nick Cave."

—*Kirkus Reviews*

"Meno has a poet's feel for small-town details, life in the joint, and the trials an ex-con faces, and he's a natural storyteller with a talent for characterization. A likable winner . . ."

—*Publishers Weekly*

JOE MENO is the author of one story collection and four novels, including *How the Hula Girl Sings* and the best-sellers *The Boy Detective Fails* and *Hairstyles of the Damned*, which was selected for the Barnes & Noble Discover Great New Writers Program and has been translated into German, Italian, Turkish, and Russian. Meno is the winner of a Nelson Algren Literary Award and is currently a professor of creative writing at Columbia College Chicago. He lives in Chicago.

TENDER
AS HELLFIRE

JOE MENO

akashic books
new york

Published by Akashic Books
Originally published in hardcover by St. Martin's Press
©1999, 2007 Joe Meno

ISBN-13: 978-1-933354-30-9
ISBN-10: 1-933354-30-5
Library of Congress Control Number: 2006936534

First Akashic Books printing

Akashic Books
PO Box 1456
New York, NY 10009
info@akashicbooks.com
www.akashicbooks.com

for my old man

acknowledgments

Thanks to Koren, who makes everything possible, Charles Everitt, Dana Albarella, C. Michael Curtis, Johnny Temple, Johanna Ingalls, Akashic Books, Dan Sinker, my friends and family, and the Columbia College Fiction Writing Department.

tenderloin

They split us up at the end of summer.

Now most people will call you a liar if you tell them a truth they don't want to hear, but I know me and I know my brother, and looking back, before our bare-legged Val left town all covered in blue bruises or Shilo got shot in the neck or the deputy just disappeared, before my brother lit a black match to all his hatred, before any of that, they decided to split us up, and I guess that's where the trouble really began.

"This place is hell. This place is shit."

Pill, my brother, nodded his head, agreeing with himself as he lit the match. There was that sharp striking sound of the match-head against the thin strip of flint, *snappppp*, then a big blossom of fire crinkling down along the match's spine. He held the flame to the end of his Marlboro and inhaled, taking a drag that crept out of the side of his mouth in a quick spurt.

We spent that first morning before the first day of school in that lousy new town smoking in the dirt, taking drags on my older brother's stolen cigarettes. We sat right behind our new mobile home, hiding in its square shadow, the trailer shining silver from its aluminum siding, refusing to sit level on its concrete blocks. Pill tapped another square out of the pack and handed it to me, then struck the flame from the match cover and lit the cigarette's tip jutting from the end of my lip.

"This place sucks," I grunted, coughing up smoke through my nose.

I was ten: which was how old I was four years ago, when all of this happened. Pill-Bug had just turned thirteen. I'm a year older now then he was at the time, which seems awful funny to me. As I think on it now, in that moment there wasn't anything better than sitting in the dusty gravel beside him, sharing a cool smoking square, not because he was especially talkative or insightful or anything like that, but he would always share what he had just stolen or show you a new wrestling move or tell you about an unfamiliar dirty word or two. My brother had on his blue stocking cap, half pulled down over his eyes, past the black scab where one eyebrow should have been. It was a wound he got lighting our neighbor's hedge on fire the day before we left Duluth.

In the shadow of that morning, Pill had his legs spread out in front of him, lying back against the concrete base of the trailer, staring at his dirty brown shoes. I had just finished buttoning up my brand-new school shirt, one of my brother's old red-and-black flannels, which was long enough for me to half-tuck in my underwear. Nothing in those stolen cigarettes or dirty clothes gave us any idea that we might both be doomed, doomed past any of our years or any of the fairly illegal things we had already done.

"Do you know what a girl's pussy smells like?" Pill asked, staring up into the cool blue sky, taking a long drag that turned the length of the cigarette gray.

I kind of shrugged my shoulders.

"Well, yes or no?" he asked, leaning forward.

"No. I guess not," I mumbled.

"It's like being stung by an electric eel. It makes you want to fuck anything that moves."

I sucked my teeth in reply.

"Get to school!" my mother shouted, shaking her fist, hollering from inside the godawful silver trailer.

A trailer: back in Duluth, we'd had a whole house to ourselves.

We even had our own rooms, but now we had to share a crummy bunk bed. My older brother got the top bunk after a short skirmish that ended up with him sitting on my neck. Also, there were shadows on our walls at night that looked like skulls. Also, there were dead mice everywhere, and even when we thought we had got rid of them all, we found some of their pink babies which we tried to feed but which died. Also, if you glanced in the bathroom mirror with the lights off, you could see ghosts standing behind you with bloody hands. Also, we discovered a stack of dirty Polaroids in a shoebox that had been left in one of the closets— they were mostly of different women lying topless in bed, which, of course, my brother kept for himself. Also, there were silverfish crawling all over the floor. Also, the nearest comic book and baseball card shop was forty-three miles away in a town called Aubrey. Also, nothing in this place was any damn good. My mother's boyfriend, French, had gotten a supervisor's position at the meatpacking plant in this town of Tenderloin and my mother packed us all up to move hundreds of miles into a lousy goddamn trailer and now we were all unhappy.

"You better be going!" my mother shouted again, knocking the gray screen door open. My brother hoisted his book bag over his shoulder and I followed, kicking up dirt as we headed toward school.

In Tenderloin they split me and my brother up good. Pill and I had been going to the same school ever since I'd been attending, but here they sent me to the elementary school and him to the high school, even though he had never really graduated eighth grade back in Duluth. He would have graduated, but he was on probation from a fistfight he'd gotten into. And then what happened was his homeroom teacher, Mrs. Henckel, this ghastly old hag who I'd say had it out for Pill-Bug, found near a dozen porno magazines and a single box of Marlboro cigarettes in his locker.

They expelled him a week before graduation, no matter how much my mother pleaded, glad as hell to be rid of him, I bet.

Three days: That's all it took before Pill lit another kid's house on fire. To be truthful, I didn't think he'd last that long. Back in Duluth, he used to get in a fight almost every day with some fool or another. My brother, Pill, he liked to get in fistfights, don't ask me why. In Tenderloin, he waited three days though before starting any trouble.

It all began at lunchtime, or that's what he told me. The high school was small enough so everyone had to eat all at once, together, in a big cafeteria painted red and white, the stupid school colors. The walls were decorated with these big paintings of a side of beef with little arms and legs, right with the school motto, *Fightin' Meat Packers*. All of these dumb kids must have been going to school together since they were born. Maybe all of them were cousins. It was the same way it is now: all the big ugly football players with their own lunch table, and the cheerleaders with their own, and the snotty student council kids, and the big red-haired, red-lipped sluts with their own rectangle. In the corner was a round table with a broken leg where all the losers and faggots were sent to sit. Pill was no faggot, no way. He was so crazy about girls that he would have masturbated every hour on the hour if he could, but he was the new kid in school, so the only spot he could find was at the loser table in the corner. Sitting at the center of the table was this huge fat girl, Candy, no shit, her name was Candy, I'm not lying, and she filled up half one side of the table, her blob of a body kind of undulating and wavering above her three trays of food, which of course was mostly snack items and several helpings of sloppy joes, and which left deep orange stains all over her fat fingers and round chin. Then there was Kenny, who rode the short bus to school; he had grabbed a kite string off an electrical wire and gotten severe brain damage. He had to ride in an electric wheelchair and wear a protective helmet all the time. People didn't like him because he used to try to run you down in the hall between classes, or sometimes, I guess, during football games, he'd ride around the track and no one would try to stop him. Beside him, there was some flitty kids and some real brainiac types who didn't even bother eating lunch because they were so worried about studying and getting good grades and getting the hell out of that town. Then there was my brother, Pill, who didn't fit anywhere there at all. He was short and dirty and mostly mean-looking. He had one eyebrow and a huge black scab in the other eyebrow's place. He wore his dirty black drawers and a gray flannel jacket and his godawful blue stocking cap that no one could convince him to take off, because his hair was growing back from the fire and there was still a bald spot big as a fist right on the crown of his head.

When Pill had almost finished lunch, an older kid, a senior with dark hair cut in a mullet, walked up to the table and stared down at him. "Hey there, you're new here, right?"

Pill nodded, not looking up.

"We were all wondering if you knew that you looked like a pussy."

My brother just lowered his head, shoveling another helping of meatloaf over his lips, trying to swallow. A few more of these older kids with their jean jackets and mullets, some with red-and-white varsity letters pinned to their dirty coats, all gathered around. Poor Candy squealed and folded in on herself. Kenny and the other losers at the table just got all quiet and pretended to be finishing their lunches.

"Hey, I just called you a pussy, pussy," the older kid with the mullet and square face grunted again. "Don't you know I'm talking to you?"

"Forget him, Rudy, he looks retarded," one of the other kids said.

"Don't you know it's ignorant to ignore someone when they're trying to talk to you?" Rudy asked.

But my brother kept eating, cleaning his plate, shaking his head to himself a little. Finally, he stood up and stared right in that bigger kid's face without saying a word. Rudy put his arm around my brother's neck, squeezing him tightly.

"Just tell me you know you're a pussy and I'll leave you alone. Go ahead. Tell me."

The one thing Pill-Bug couldn't stand, quiet and crazy as I knew him to be, was anyone touching him or his stuff. He snarled his lips and clenched his fists, kind of staring at this other kid's jugular vein, gripping a plastic fork in his trembling hand. A teacher, that day's lunch room monitor, stared over at them both, eyeballing them hard. Rudy held Pill there, my poor brother almost foaming at the mouth, as the teacher pointed at them, half-heartedly trying to break it up.

"Get back to your seats," the lunch monitor mumbled in a lazy tone. Rudy smiled and nodded, then shoved my brother again.

"Pussy," Rudy whispered, and quickly swiped the blue stocking cap from my brother's still-bald head.

Oh Jesus.

My poor brother must have just froze with shock and horror. His blue eyes must have went wide and shallow as he glanced around the lunch room. Everyone was looking at the huge blot of red skin where his curly black hair hadn't grown back. All these goddamn cheerleaders and sluts and student council kids and football players were mumbling and giggling and pointing right at him, their laughter echoing like pins and needles in his brain.

"You will all die!" he shouted. Then he let out a howl and ran through the lunch room doors, screaming like a madman, down the hall, knocking over a garbage can, tearing a homecoming poster off the wall. He ran right into the boy's bathroom, hissed and swung his fist through the first mirror he could see, and then jumped out the window into some hedges and ran across the football field, back toward the trailer park, still screaming and tearing up anything that fell in his path.

Or maybe not.

Maybe I don't really know what his first day was like. I mean, I wasn't even there. I guess there were the things he said and the rest of the stuff people told me, so everything else I guess I've had to make up. It might have happened that way or not. I guess I'm still trying to figure it all out is what I mean.

I do know that my own first day was just as lousy.

I was awful happy at first because the fifth grade teacher was real pretty. Her name was Miss Nelson. Boy, her legs were as long as my whole body, and during the whole damn class, all I could think about was her legs. She just kept smiling and laughing and sitting on the corner of her desk and talking about getting good grades and not being late, just sitting there being nothing but beautiful. Her hair was all straight and black and long down her back. Her eyes were blue and twice as big behind nice black glasses. She wore this short flowered dress that hung just over her knees. I was in heaven, heaven, until she took out the fifth grade roster and started calling out names for attendance. I kind of slunk in my chair, shaking my head, trying to make myself disappear. Miss Nelson worked her way through the alphabet. There was damn near half-a-dozen Johnnys and Jimmys and Jennys in my class. Then she passed the Is and then the Js and then the Ks and then her perfect pink mouth opened like a rose when she said my name.

"Dough?"

It made my heart sink in my chest. Her eyes scanned the room, over the rounded heads of all the ten-year-olds, through the forest of pigtails and flattops, right to me. Her pink lips parted a little smile as she called my name.

"Dough Lunt? Is your name Dough?"

Everyone in the class turned around and stared right at me, all these stupid Johnnys and Jimmys and Jennys, all of them. I kind of raised my head just enough to nod and then slumped back down to the desk.

"Please say 'Present' if you're here, Dough."

Her eyes suddenly seemed mean and black. Her eyebrows cocked over her eyeglass frames as she stared down at me.

"Present," I murmured, and dropped my head between my arms, feeling my heart shriveling up in my chest.

"You're new here, aren't you?" she asked.

Jesus. It was bad enough all these morons knew my name, now she was going to introduce me. I nodded slowly and stared at Miss Nelson's face for some sort of reprieve. But no.

"Why don't we welcome Dough by giving him a nice 'Hello'?"

The whole class let out a sigh and the palest, weakest chorus of voices rose from the room.

"Hello, Dough."

A girl with three pigtails in her hair, sitting next to me, squinted and stared.

"What type of name is that?"

I didn't know so I shrugged my shoulders. My old man had been some sort of madman to insist on such a name: I wasn't named after some famous relative, and neither was my poor brother. We had been in some uncountable number of fistfights because of our lousy names, which had been part of my father's plan. Our names were like two huge magnets that hung around our necks, attracting all sorts of trouble, I guess.

"I don't think that's a name," this girl said with a frown.

I turned and stared her hard in the eyes. Her eyes were brown and kind of crossed. Her hair was blond and pulled so tightly in those three rubber bands that her forehead looked stretched. She smelled mostly like pee and a little like dirt.

"You live in the trailer park?" she whispered.

I tried to ignore her. "No. Just be quiet."

"You like living in the trailer park? My father says there's nothing but trash living out there but I'd love to live there. I think it would be like living in space."

I shook my head slowly. What was wrong with these people? They were all lunatics. Finally, Miss Nelson finished off the class roster and began writing something on the board. Her white slip showed between her legs as she reached up on her toes. I sighed to myself, wondering what Miss Nelson would look like in the nude.

"Did you come from Nevada?" the girl beside me asked. "My father says everyone's crazy out there."

"Do you ever shut up?"

Miss Nelson turned around, staring right through the rows of sleeping faces, right at me. She glanced down at the roster and nodded.

"Dough, do you have something to share with the rest of the class?"

"This girl here won't shut up."

"Lottie, is that true?"

Lottie, this piss-girl with three blond pigtails, just smiled and shrugged her shoulders, staring at me like I was crazy.

"Both of you will be quiet from now on, understood?"

I nodded, then looked down at my paper and began to draw a gladiator beheading a stick figure with three pigtails.

I came home from my first day of school, dragging my book bag

in the dirt. The only thing I did like about living in the trailer park
was that I didn't have to mow the lawn. Mowing the lawn was a
pain because the mower burnt your legs, but now there was nothing except gravel all around us and dirt. My mother had tried to lay
out some orange flowerpots around the front, but she wasn't fool-
ing anyone. The trailer park was like a stab wound in all our hearts,
and that wouldn't be changed by any number of flowerpots.

In front of the trailer, my mother's boyfriend, French, was
working on his big black 1972 Impala he had on cement blocks.
The car itself was a real beauty, but it was all gutted out, its insides
strewn about the dust, disconnected and hopeless as hell—the
engine had never even turned over. French had bought it from
some slimeball back in Duluth who promised to help him rebuild
it, but then the guy split town as soon as French paid the car off.
Now old French had to walk to work. The plant was only a mile
or so away, and most days he could get a ride with someone if he
stood out on the road and hitched. My mother had her own car,
a blue Corolla hatchback with rusted-out wheel wells and a dangling muffler that she drove to her job at the beauty parlor. Her
car was in a poor state too. My old man probably turned over in
his grave every time he heard that muffler drag. He had been good
with tools. He would have been too proud to let the muffler drag
on his wife's car, but none of that mattered too much now, con-
sidering how terrible everything else had become.

"Hey there, Dough, feel like giving me a hand? Hold the
flashlight for me?"

French was bent over the hood of the car. His face was greased
up and sweaty. He held a yellow flashlight in one hand and an
open can of beer in the other. French was the cause of many of my
troubles. He was a square guy, really, the least dangerous of all my
mother's boyfriends, but there was no way I was about to offer
help to the person responsible for making us move.

"I got homework, French."

"All right, chief, that's what I like to see. Smart man like you hitting the books. Your mother will be proud."

"I guess."

Mom had a big dinner cooked for us, on account of our first day being at new schools. She had made meatloaf with a raw egg cooked right in the middle and a horrible gray spinach salad or something hellacious like that, but both me and my brother passed and just went to our room, lying in our lousy new beds, half the size of our old beds, neither of us uttering a word.

"You boys all right in there? Not hungry tonight?" my mother shouted through the thin wood door.

"Ate at school," Pill-Bug lied, shaking his head.

"I got homework," I grunted, turning on my belly.

At night there were loud silver-legged crickets screeching outside our tiny square window, singing desperate in any direction, just as sad and hopeless as us, as we stared up into the darkness. I fell asleep in my school clothes, watching a daddy longlegs crossing the ceiling on its tiptoes.

The next day, Pill and me ate some doughnuts for breakfast and walked to school without saying a word until we got to the intersection: It was where he had to walk three blocks to the high school and me one street over to the elementary school.

"This place sure sucks," I kind of mumbled.

Pill nodded. "This town is full of assholes."

Just then I noticed he had a red stocking cap on instead of his trusty old blue hat. He always wore his blue hat. "Hey, where's your blue hat?" I asked him.

"I lost it."

"Lost it? But—"

"I said I lost it, okay?" He heaved his book bag over his shoul-

der and turned down the block toward the high school. That's
when I knew there was going to be trouble. His eyes had that faraway look in them like he was thinking, like he was looking ahead
to something that he hadn't done yet, but knew he ought not to
do.

At school, Pill wandered through his classes until lunch. He
bought a plate of mashed potatoes and some french fries, then
took a seat at the reject table in the corner. Billy Harlo, one of
those fat freckled kids who had probably been picked on since he
was born, giggled to himself as Pill sat down. Billy Harlo got
picked on not only because he was fat but because he had chronic
nosebleeds. Pill-Bug didn't pay the fat kid any mind.

About midway through the lunch hour, the same older kid,
Rudy, came right up to the loser table, this time waving my brother's blue hat right in his damn face. Pill kind of ignored him for a
while, then he began snarling and growling like a sick dog, snatch-
ing at the cap as Rudy kind of jerked it away. It was awful.
Everyone in the cafeteria was watching and grinning, even Billy
Harlo and the rest of the reject kids, because for once, no one was
picking on them. "What are you gonna do, pussy? Huh? What are
you gonna do?" Pill looked away, then leapt to his feet, tripping
over his seat. He slid, his arm landing in his mashed potatoes, his
whole shirt now covered with brown gravy. Rudy laughed, chuck-
ling as he said, "What? It was just a joke. Why do you gotta get all
psycho? Relax." He handed my brother the dirty blue hat, walking away, high-fiving his friends. Pill looked down, gripping his
hat, then ran out through the cafeteria doors again, tearing posters
and announcements off the walls as he went. He hurried through
the front doors and disappeared somewhere down the street, still
shouting.

The second day for me wasn't much better. There was some sort of math quiz everyone else seemed to know about, but all I was interested in doing was trying to stare up Miss Nelson's dress. So instead of answering the math questions, I drew a real sweet picture of a tank fighting a man with a rhinoceros head, right on the quiz paper, and handed that in to the teacher instead. Miss Nelson just shook her head, marking a big red *F* at the top of the page with a frown, and in that moment, I kind of knew that anything between us was going to be hopeless. The pigtailed girl, Lottie, talked my head off that day, saying something about how her father's chickens were all dying, one by one, waking up with their necks wrung, then she told me about her older sister, Susie, who was pregnant and wouldn't tell anyone who the father was because she didn't want their old man to go out and kill the poor fool. I fell asleep at some point while she was chattering and missed some important information about world geography, which I was sure I probably needed to know for another upcoming quiz. Walking home from school that day, none of these dumb kids had comic books or porno magazines or cigarettes or anything, so I walked by myself on one side of the street, then down to the culvert by the trailer park so I could just be alone and think.

There was nobody else around the ditch, so I laid on my back and put my books under my head and practiced spitting. I spat a goober up in the air and practiced catching it, then spitting it again. The grass was soft and kind of wet; it still smelled like summer—green and warm. There were some old pages of a newspaper drifting in the water and an old tire that floated past. I looked around and noticed suddenly that this was a place of death. There was a dead sheep that looked like it had strayed off from somewhere and laid down right beside a gray metal irrigation pipe. Its eyes were cold and black and its ivory teeth were spread apart over its red gums. There were tiny insects creeping all around it. The sheep's wool was full of brambles and dried leaves and there, caught in one of its teeth, was a bright yellow flower, looking like a prize. Under the irrigation pipe, right along the surface of the water, there were some dead birds, tiny yellow sparrows and shiny black birds, dozens of them, maybe almost twenty, all with their wings spread open, drowned beside one another. I talked to them for a while and asked them about my dad, because he was dead too, and then I walked along the ditch for about a mile, staring into the gray water, and finally turned back home. I didn't want to go on back to the trailer and have to talk to my mom or French about school, so I waited down by the culvert until it was dark, crawled in through the sliding window to our bedroom, and let my mom think I had come home from school early and fallen asleep so she'd just pat me on my head and let me be.

But my brother wasn't home. I laid there in the bunk bed all alone until my mother came in. Her lips were warm when she kissed me goodnight and made me think everything would be all right. Those kinds of things I don't like to mention too often because they always make you look stupid when someone else finds out, being kissed goodnight by your mom and all, but it always gave me a nice feeling I could dream a nice dream to.

The day after that, Pill and me walked to school together. He was wearing his blue hat again but by then I was too worried about Miss Nelson and fifth grade and having to listen to this girl, Lottie, ramble to me all day, that I wasn't paying much attention to my brother and his problems. I did notice he was carrying a black plastic bag, all shiny and heavy and stiff with something, just holding it there by his side. I stared at my older brother as we stood at our intersection, eyeing each other hard.

"What the hell's in the bag?" I grunted.

He just kept staring at me, then muttered, "Don't let anyone push you around, Dough. You understand? Don't ever let anyone push you around."

I nodded and walked down the block a little. Then I turned around to see him, but he had already walked off and it was too late for me to do anything because I could hear the first bell already ringing.

He didn't go right off to school.

He stood in front of a white A-frame house, smoking fever-ishly. A gray cloud trailed out from between his lips and ran around the end of the square jammed between his two fingers. He stood under a wilting maple tree, turning the book of matches over and over again in his pocket. The black plastic bag was sitting at his feet. He squinted a little, smoking hard. Pill had gotten into a fistfight with nearly every kid back home in Duluth. He had plenty of teeth knocked out, his nose broken, clumps of his hair torn out; Diffy Morrison once sicced his dog on Pill and he had to get fifty-two stitches from it. He had been smacked by my mother's old boyfriend, Joe Brown, at least half a dozen times, hit by the school bus once, not to mention getting his hair and eye-brows burned off the day before we left Duluth. He was a tough kid and no one knew it better than me, but this was different, he wasn't in Duluth and he wasn't fistfighting just one bully. He hated the whole town already, and when the fat girls and the retards at the round table in the cafeteria laugh at you, it gives you a certain feeling that makes you want to stare at things by yourself and maybe smoke a Marlboro for a while. He had something awful to do and he knew it. He wasn't a moron; he wasn't a mon-ster either; maybe people like to think that when you know you've got something awful to do, you just don't think about it first, but that wasn't true. He had something awful he was about to do and he knew it and maybe that's what made it worse.

For a long time, he stared at the blank silver mailbox, turning the book of matches over in his palm again and again. *LaDell*, the mailbox read. The driveway was empty. No one was home. Their grass glimmered green with the morning light. Pill stood there a long while just thinking and smoking. The smoke hung around his face. The matches became soft with his sweat. He lit another cigarette and took a long drag. He stared at the shiny green grass, seeing how each blade moved like a whisper, like a single sigh, like a curse word spoken over and over again. He flicked the cigarette into the grass, picked up the black plastic bag, slammed the red metal flag down on the mailbox, and walked up to the nice white porch.

Snap.

Snappppppp.

Snapppppppppppppp.

The bell clanged: It was already lunch time.

Pill nodded to himself and walked inside the high school cafeteria, holding his hands inside his pockets as he marched down the rows and rows of brown tables and chairs, kind of sweating a little along his forehead. His eyes were shiny and black like he was about to cry, but he wasn't; his blue cap was nearly pulled down over his eyebrow and the hard black scab. He pushed through the line of kids in their dull flannel school clothes, the jocks in blue jeans and yellow-haired girls in denim overalls who were all giggling and pulling on each other's sweaters. He got his food and walked past them all, right up to the back round table.

When Rudy LaDell and his buddies walked past, Pill looked up from his lunch and glared.

"What? You got something to say, pussy?" Rudy asked, but Pill only smiled and looked back down at his awful food.

After school, Pill waited in the parking lot, watching all the groups of kids hurrying into their beat-up cars or onto the bus. He was waiting for Rudy LaDell. When the older kid appeared, his jean jacket tight against his shoulders, Pill watched as he climbed into his rebuilt black Camaro, the screech of some unidentifiable heavy-metal guitar solo echoing from its speakers. Rudy slipped on a pair of sunglasses, lit a joint, and began laughing with his friends, who all piled into the backseat. When he saw my brother standing there staring, he stopped talking to the bright-eyed girl leaning against the driver's side door and stared back, flipping him the bird. Pill looked away as Rudy LaDell's Camaro peeled out, the back end of the car fishtailing a little as it flew over the gravelly road.

Pill hiked his book bag over his shoulder and began to follow the small groups of kids along the culvert, away from the shadow of the high school, past the wasteland of the supermarket and video store and 7-Eleven, then he turned, walking a couple of feet behind two freshmen girls in tight jean skirts. He watched the shape their legs made as they walked, laughing, glancing over their shoulders. When they stopped to share a cigarette at the pizza place, one of them pretending to play an arcade machine out front, they rolled their eyes as my brother walked past, and the other one whispered, *"Maybe he has a staring problem."* Pill ignored them and headed back toward the culvert, sitting beside an irrigation pipe to have a smoke, throwing a stone at a bird picking apart a beetle.

By the time he made his way down the rows of small white houses along the east side of Main, he could see two firetrucks parked in the middle of the street, their lights flashing, a cloud of smoke drifting noiselessly in the air. A couple of other kids from the high school were standing around in a circle gawking, although the fire had been put out a few hours ago. With the rest of the small crowd across the street, Pill stood and looked at the dark black spot where a porch had once been, the wood now molted and black, the rest of the house still intact though glistening with water and singed with smoke. *"Wow,"* one girl with bangs muttered, *"that's really awful."* Silently, my brother stared across the street at the ruined porch for a while longer, then turned, walking slowly back toward the culvert, disappearing in the high grass and weeds, dragging his book bag behind him through the murk.

A few days later, Rudy LaDell became a ghost. His muscle car would just appear from out of nowhere, him smoking a joint in the driver's seat, watching me and my brother walking home, or every so often it would be waiting in the parking lot of the convenience store when we'd go to try and buy smokes, or it would even show up when I was playing in the ditch all alone; I'd look up and there would be his black Camaro, the same song, the same stupid metal riff blaring from its blown speakers, like a kind of phantom, I guess. I would glare at him sitting there in the driver's seat, and sooner or later it would be quiet and the car would be gone. I really don't know what happened to him except that he didn't fuck with my brother again. Of that, I'm pretty sure.

Going back to that night, the night of the fire, I almost forgot that a deputy sheriff came by and asked Pill if he knew anything about who had started it. Of course, Pill said he didn't know a thing. When the deputy left, unconvinced, my mom began shouting and Pill hurried off to his room. I knew at once what he had done, but I wasn't mad at him for it, just sad, I guess, sad that he was already in trouble again.

"Did you light that fire?" I asked him as we were lying in our bunk beds. "Was that you?"

He turned in the bunk above mine. His breath was short and shallow as he cleared his throat.

"No," he whispered. "No, that wasn't me. I didn't have nothing to do with it."

God, I wanted to believe him. More than anything in the world, I wanted to pretend he was telling me the truth. He was my only brother and he had never lied to me about anything important in my whole life before. He had always been the one person to tell me things everyone else was afraid to say or thought I shouldn't know, like how my old man had died or how to make it with a girl or how to stand up for myself no matter what bullshit my mother or teachers gave me, but this was all something different, this was something new. Him lying to me right then was so terrible that I thought I ought to forgive him for it right away. Maybe he hadn't meant for it to happen like it had. Maybe he'd made a mistake. Either way, he didn't say another word, just rolled over and pulled the covers up over his head.

But that's what I meant by what I said.

Them splitting us up is where all the trouble really began.

kiss of soft gravel

The only girl I ever loved was Val. At the time, she was twenty-eight and paid to babysit us every other Friday night. I don't remember much about her but her legs, which were the long, white reflection of beauty. The shape of her naked form would make me want to break something. I wouldn't know what else to do. It's always been like that for me. Didn't you ever love someone you knew you couldn't have? People might call you stupid but there's nothing you can do to help it. My lust for Miss Nelson, my fifth grade teacher, would go on for another few weeks, until she shot me enough dirty looks to make me cringe and shrink in my poor wooden seat, urging me to draw a picture of her being bombarded by a squadron of WWII fighters on a geography exam. But Val. Her blue eyes made me want to set the whole world on fire.

I don't think we were supposed to know this, but my mother and her boyfriend, French, liked to party, having cocktails or smoking dope or doing lines of coke with other couples from the plant, and they needed somewhere to send me and my brother every other Friday night. Pill was thirteen and old enough not to need a babysitter, but both of us were prone to getting in trouble, and between us lighting stuff on fire and shouting and running around trying to murder each other and my mother screaming at us and French walking around in his underwear, I don't think we were much appreciated by our neighbors. No one came right out and said anything, but a dumb, listless stare can tell you a lot of things ignorant people are afraid to say. So my mother and French paid this young truck-stop waitress at the other end of the trailer park to keep us in her spare bedroom every other Friday night and make sure we didn't burn or steal anything we couldn't afford to repay ourselves.

Almost every other Friday night, my mother would give me and Pill a brown grocery bag of our clothes and toothbrushes, then send us down the gravel road to Val's silver trailer that was round and looked like a kind of space capsule. Pill was never happy about going. He hated Tenderloin, and being cooped up inside on a Friday night, when he could be out knocking mail-boxes over or pissing someone off, must have burned him up pretty bad. He'd kind of sulk behind me with his hands in his pockets as we'd cross the court to her trailer. I'd wipe my nose clean with the back of my hand and then knock on her screen door. Val's trailer was always lit up with a string of white Christmas lights. I don't know if she put them up for Christmas or not, but she sure never took them down. Her bare legs would appear there behind the screen. I don't know what it was about her legs; she was tall, really tall, taller than French. Her legs were just so long that I'd kind of whistle to myself every time I'd see them. I mean, it wasn't like I'd know what to do with them if I had the chance, but there was something inside my chest that would light up like a match whenever she'd answer the door. Her hair was blond and cut short, and she'd usually be in her work uniform, which was a yellow dress with a white apron, her hair all done up with a white paper crown. She'd lead us inside and pat my head and lick her finger and stick it in Pill's ear. He liked her too, he really did, but most of the time we were there he was in a mean mood. Her trailer always smelled the way I thought a girl should, like cigarettes and baby powder. Her breath was always hot and musty, moving over a wad of pink bubble gum. Her mouth would leave bright red lipstick marks on the spotted white glasses she drank gin from. There was nothing I wanted more than to touch her and have her kiss my forehead and let me fall asleep in her bed without anyone else, alone sleeping in her golden arms all night.

And maybe after we got there, she'd pour us some RC Cola in some giveaway glasses that she'd gotten at a fast-food joint, or maybe she'd light a cigarette as she got undressed, but every Friday night we were there, she would strip down to her smooth white skin behind this Oriental screen decorated with a yellow tiger and tie her red Oriental robe around her middle, tucking the edges between her breasts. Seeing her when she appeared in her robe would make my teeth hum in my head.

After that, she'd take a bath. Honest to God, she'd take a bath right while we were there. She'd close this small wooden door and slip into her pink bathtub and take a goddamn bath. It was as though we didn't have a choice but to try and look. Pill always got to go first, then me. Our greasy faces would smear against the silver keyhole, unable to breathe as her naked shoulders appeared in our eyes. My face would get all red and hot and once I think I nearly passed out when she suddenly stood and stepped out of the tub and I gazed upon her naked form, her smooth white belly, her wide hips that slipped down to form the most perfect V I'd ever seen. I nearly blacked out right there but Pill grabbed me by the back of the shirt and held me up by my collar. His face wouldn't get all red or anything, he'd just get kind of quiet and mad. Heck, I knew why, he was three whole years older than me and he thought he shouldn't even be there. But since I knew this was the closest I was going to get to a naked woman, I didn't ever complain.

When her bare white legs appeared from behind the bathroom door, clouded by steam, still a little wet, she'd shout at us for gawking at her. She'd have her hair wrapped up in a pink towel on the top of her head and she'd be wearing that crazy Chinese robe, all black and red and white and flowery; she'd tuck her legs beneath her and take a seat on the sofa. Maybe she'd turn on the radio or something. Maybe she'd put on a nice record by Patsy Cline and stare out the screen windows into the dull blue night. By then, Pill would be getting all kinds of anxious. He was a boy with sex on the brain, and so maybe Val would send him out to go pick up our dinner. That was fine with me, because then it would be just me and Val in the trailer alone. She'd unwrap her hair and let it fall over her white shoulders, or maybe she'd blow dry it a little, then go behind that black screen and pull on a tight gray T-shirt or some overalls. Anything looked good on her, I swear. We'd sit on her sofa and watch the night come up, the blue sky giving way to blackness, me leaning in close to smell the shampoo and soap evaporating off her body; sweet and heavy like perfume, it would just hang like a cloud in the air. Maybe then she'd ask me something nice like, "How many girlfriends do you have?" or, "How come you're such a heartbreaker?" and then Pill-Bug would return with some fried chicken or hamburgers or something from down the road. We'd all eat, laughing and giggling and throwing food and having the best time of our lives. Well, maybe not Pill. Or Val. But being with the both of them felt all right to me.

Anyway, later, we'd go out on Val's porch. She'd pour herself a drink and keep patting me on the head and giving me wet kisses on the cheek. We'd watch the last of the fireflies glowing in the tall brown grass and listen across the courtyard to where our own trailer was ringing with the unfamiliar sounds of laughter. We'd all lie down on her porch and drink gin and water, which isn't such a strong drink, I guess, but enough to make your head swim if you happen to be lying next to the beauty of your life. "My men," Val would laugh, hugging us both. Pill would try to ignore her, he'd just keep drinking the booze, kind of frowning, but when a nice lady like that puts her finger wet with spit in your ear, you can't help but feel a certain way. "My two men, that's all I need."

My face would feel warm against her belly where my head lay just below her breasts.

"Val, will you marry me when I'm older?" I'd ask.

"Sure thing, darling."

At that moment, I couldn't figure there was anything better in the world. Maybe Val would give us some firecrackers to light off, or maybe we'd go for a walk down the road and watch the brown toads scurrying from one side to the other. By then it would be dark out and late. Val would make us brush our teeth and wash our faces. She'd let us fall asleep on her sofa, listening to some old records or watching her tiny black-and-white television. Then she'd help us into the big white bed in the spare room, the bed that smelled like the soft, wrinkled part of her neck where there'd always be a greasy dab of perfume. Her head would hang over us as her robe would drop open a little, showing the space just above her heart, the smooth white plain that I knew she shared with truck drivers and cowboys and men who drove pickups. Her mouth would swell as she'd smile and wink us a goodnight, and then I'd reach up and kiss her on the soft side of her red mouth. That moment, right there, is still what I think about when I think about love. The soft side of someone's mouth.

Pill would lie on his belly, burying his face in her pillows. I would lie on my back, and then we would hold our breath and listen, because there would always be some cowboy coming over to fuck, because even as young as I was, I knew that's all they wanted anyway. Pill would flip and flop around, frustrated, I guess. He'd grit his teeth all night and shake his head and then we'd hear a pickup or big block engine Chevy die outside, then the boots, scrape-scrape-scraping over the gravel, the bare-knuckled knock on the door, the screen door would slide open, they would be whispering and giggling, maybe there would be the sharp kiss of glasses striking together, then it would stop, then it would be so quiet that I could hear my brother's congested chest rising and falling with each shallow breath. Maybe there would be the squeak of furniture, of wood against tile, or metal against metal spring, but sooner of later I'd slip out of bed and stare out the tiny gold keyhole, out into the dimly lit darkness. From only a few feet away, my whole world would come apart.

Val's long white legs might be straddled around this cowboy's middle, his shirt might be unbuttoned, and her mouth might be moving over his mouth, maybe she'd be on her back or bent over the same sofa, but they would be fucking, not gently, not like a whisper, not like a kiss, they would be fucking hard and tearing at each other's clothes and scratching and pulling and rubbing their bodies together in a way that made me hate her and him and everything about them both. Maybe I'd try to go back to sleep, maybe I'd hide my head under some of her blankets and listen to them fucking all night. These men, these truckers and cowboys, had some sort of endurance I couldn't even imagine. Maybe they were just like Pill and me, but older, full of the same frustration and rage, and so they needed to let it out somehow, through some-one else's soft body. Those men I hated more than anything I've ever hated in my life.

Those men would appear every other Friday night as soon as we had been tucked in. Every other Friday night another cowboy or trucker would come over and make time with Val, and only once did I know that she ever got herself in a bind.

One night a big blond-haired cowboy in tight jeans came knocking on Val's screen door. He was the one with the sandy-colored cowboy hat, the silver-toed boots, and the blue Western shirt. He was drunk, stumbling as he climbed out of his truck, and so poor Val refused to let him in.

"Just open the door for a second, Val, honey. Just for a second." The cowboy's voice was sweet and cool. His eyes were red and nearly crossed with sincerity.

"Not tonight, baby," Val said, pulling her robe tight around her waist. "Go on home."

"Just a second," he groaned. "Please, honey, just fer a single kiss." He clawed at the thin screen like an animal, kneeling in front of the door.

"Don't make a fool outta yourself. Go on home, baby. You're drunk and ornery. And I'm not in the mood for any of that."

The cowboy pulled his sandy-colored hat down over his eyes. He yanked himself to his feet, leaning against the door, and tore a big knife from the side of his boot.

"Looks like I'm going to have to invite myself in then."

He dug the blade into the screen, yanking the knife down and across in a big L-shape. Val let out a scream and I shot up in bed, rustling my brother awake. Val backed away from the front door as the cowboy smiled, slowly stalking her.

"I just want a kiss," he grunted, tripping through the big tear in the door. "That's it."

He held the knife out before him, the silver knife with its smooth ivory bone handle, grinning like a sick dog.

"Now you ain't so proud, are ya?" he snorted.

Val backed into the kitchen, fumbling behind her for some kind of weapon—a knife, a screwdriver, anything. The cowboy kept smiling and grinning, moving closer. By now, Pill and I had opened the spare bedroom door and were standing right there a few feet from it all, unable to muster a single word.

"Go back to bed, boys," Val whispered, still pleasant, still calm. "Henry and I are only playing."

But my brother didn't move. He stood in the doorway, staring at the cowboy's sweaty face.

"Don't move a muscle, boys," the cowboy grunted, turning toward us a little. "You both stand right there."

My hands ached with sweat. My whole head felt light and then heavy and then light again. Val had a tiny screwdriver in her hand but she was shaking. Her hips shivered against the kitchen counter. Her blue eyes were glimmering with big silver tears.

The cowboy took one step closer and then knocked the screwdriver right from Val's shaky hand.

"Don't you ever tease a man," the cowboy said, putting the knife against her wrist. "Don't ever play a man for a fool." He reached his hand down between the folds of her robe, right between her breasts where her heart must have been beating like a scared rabbit. My mouth was dry and hard with fear. I felt my own knees shaking. Pill looked ready to cry. His hands were clenched tight at his side.

"Don't either of you boys move," he grunted. He stood in front of her, hulking her in his shadow. There was no sound in the whole trailer. No one was breathing. No one could breathe. Then a bit of gravel rattled outside in the dark. A single shot of gravel flew from the ground and ricocheted against the side of someone else's trailer, then another, the rumble of loose gravel echoing as two double-beams crossed the inside of Val's trailer, lighting up the cowboy's face. Then a pickup truck door opened and two boots slid across the dirt and up the steps and then I heard the single sweetest word I'll ever remember: "Val?"

Still all silent inside.

"Val?!"

Then a trucker stepped through the gape in the screen, a big square-faced man in blue coveralls. His name was scribbled on a patch on one side of his jumpsuit: *Buddy*. His hair was black and disheveled a bit. He had a jug of wine in one hand and a single daisy in the other. His jaw set tight in his mouth as he stepped inside and saw Val pressed up hard against her own kitchen counter.

"You best put that knife down, chief," Buddy whispered, setting the wine and flower down on the sofa. "Before you end up cutting yourself."

The cowboy turned and glared. There were no other words needed right there. The cowboy turned and lunged at poor Buddy, taking a wide, drunken swipe at him, cleaving the front of his coveralls. Buddy slammed the cowboy hard in the throat with a solid punch, knocking his sandy-colored hat off, then Buddy dove right at him, shoving the cowboy over the sofa. The two men landed on top of each other, growling and cursing, Buddy on top, trying to wrestle the knife away from the cowboy, who spat and drooled and hissed like a snake. Buddy landed a few more blows, smacking the cowboy's nose, but then something happened that will always stick in my head because of how awful it all was. The blade of the knife ran straight through Buddy's right palm, straight through, then clanked dully to the floor. Buddy howled, gripping his wrist; he backed away, bowing over in pain. The cowboy picked up his knife and ran out, dove into his truck, and disappeared. He went right back into the dark night that had made him drunk and evil to begin with. His hat was still lying on the floor. Buddy kind of tumbled into the bathroom, gritting his teeth in pain. He held his hand under the sink, running the water over his wound. Val came up behind him and began kissing his neck and saying, "I'm sorry, so sorry, baby," and nuzzled her head against his big shoulders. He wrapped a big pink towel around his hand, shutting off the faucet while Val hurried me and my brother back into the spare bedroom, then locked us in. Her face was as white as her sheets and her blue eyes were swimming with tears. She hadn't said a word to us. She was still shaking. From the keyhole we watched as she quickly stepped back into the bathroom.

As usual, they began making it: Right in that bathroom, Val fell to her knees and unzipped the man's coveralls and then closed the bathroom door. Then there was the unmistakable sound of that man and Val, like every other Friday night, cinched together, bare and cold, their bodies pressed against the wood door, creating a kind of friction that hurt my heart and teeth and tongue. That was when I wished both those men had been killed right there, that was when I didn't care anymore that this man was hurt saving Val. This man with the hole in his hand was no different from any of the other men who would come over after Val had put us to bed. He still had that same dumb look in his eyes. That's what I hated most about all those men. They weren't any smarter than me. But there was nothing I could do about any of it. I was a dumb kid and all these men had snakeskin boots and red pickups with gun racks, and what could I possibly offer her? How could I make her feel the way they made her feel, held down against the sofa, naked and used and bare? My same brother was already asleep, snoring with the same frustration and hate. I thought of those long white legs and truckers and cowboys and trailers and the whole town, and not just the town, but all of it, everything that hangs over your head when you feel like a man but still look like a kid.

All that was too much for me. This man and Val were making it right outside the door or on the sofa or in the kitchen, fucking with a kind of rhythm so mean that I slipped on my jeans and shoes and climbed out the spare bedroom window, down into the gravel, skidding past the fading light shot from Val's black-and-white TV. I stared at this man's pickup, same as the rest, with their Valiants, Monte Carlos, big Fords, and Chevys. I reached down into the dirt and picked up the sharpest rock I could find and lit a match to what was welling up in me all night. I let that rock fly hard and straight, busting the rearview mirror and the headlights, scratching the deeply honed doors and kicking in the silverchromed grille, until Val's porch light flicked on and I disappeared back into the darkness, back through the window, and back into her soft, sleepless bed, still shaking with rage. Maybe the trucker cussed or shouted and then took off, maybe he stayed and took his anger out on her again, maybe they laid together not touching each other or even uttering a word, both wishing he had left, but the next morning the trucker was gone and I couldn't have been any happier.

When Pill and I finally rolled out of bed, we got dressed and sat at her small kitchen table. We wolfed down big helpings of French toast and burnt bacon. No one talked. Val stared hard into my eyes and didn't say a damn word; she looked me in my face and then turned away, cold and silent. I didn't mind her being mad. As long as the trucker was gone, she could be as mad as she liked. I know that sounds selfish, but she had to know there was nothing between her and that man but the both of them being desperate, and me busting up his headlights only put a kind of picture to all of that. We packed our stuff back up in our grocery bag and stepped outside. The trailer park was bright and silver with dust. Maybe I turned around and said goodbye, or maybe I was mean and stone-faced and stepped out onto her porch without muttering a thing, but Val stopped me and put her hand on my shoulder and looked down into my eyes and said something like: "You're gonna end up hurtin' someone with all that anger, Dough. You're gonna end up hurtin' yourself and someone you love with a temper like that."

More than anything I felt like crying, but I didn't, because Pill was standing by me and would have never let me live it down, and so I nodded and turned away and me and my brother walked across the lots of mobile homes, disappearing back into our own bleak hell, kicking rocks at each other without saying another goddamn word.

the sounds of midnight

At night the trailer park belonged to blood and tigers.

For some reason I began to suffer the worst nightmares I'd ever had in my life. Nightmares that made me sweat right through the white sheets of my bunk bed, nightmares that made my blood run cold and kept my older brother up with cries of my terror. I would lie awake and imagine that there were things there in the dark armed with claws and fangs, animals with rabies, animals like spitting snakes, horrors Pill used to try to scare me with. All he'd have to do was whisper the word "tiger" at night from the top bunk while I was trying to fall asleep and I'd nearly wet my bed. In Duluth, it had been quiet at night. Here, in Tenderloin, I was surrounded by the unfamiliar sound of nature around us all the time: crickets chirping outside our bedroom window, coyotes howling, birds screeching in the dark. Jungle cats, slick, unthinking, leopards and cheetahs and tigers, began to invade my dreams. They would lunge at me in my nightmares and snap my neck. I would wake up and feel their claws around my throat. I would lie there, pretending to be dead, sure some wild animal was lurking outside my window, searching the night for the sound of my heart.

During the day, I tried to sleep in class. But Lottie, the slow girl who sat beside me, the one with the three or four pigtails that pulled the skin on her face tight across her forehead, well, this girl began to annoy me more and more. Her constant jabbering was always getting me in trouble with Miss Nelson and my grades were beginning to suffer. So I used to just lay my head down on my desk and stare through my fingers at her; tired from not sleeping at night, I would watch her tiny mouth make huge spit bubbles and kissy-faces. Her tongue would shoot in and out until I would kick her or pull her hair. This girl, Lottie, wasn't all bad, she would let me cheat off her tests most of the time, but she wasn't much smarter than me, so it didn't really help. At recess, she would ask me to play a game and instead of tag, I would give her an Indian burn. I guess I pulled her hair and spat at her because I thought I could. She was a girl, and as girls go she was probably the worst of the bunch. She was the kind of girl who other girls in class hated and picked on, the girl who boys pushed down on the playground to cop a feel off of, the girl who teachers ignored because she was so slow and awkward that somehow there wasn't any room left to pity her.

One day, right in the middle of class, only three weeks after we had started school, Lottie stood up and started screaming. I hadn't even been paying attention. Maybe I'd been staring out the window dreaming, or maybe I had fallen asleep feeling the tiger's jaws around my neck. I turned and faced something that made me shiver.

"Miss Nelson . . . ?!"

Lottie was crying, holding her hands between her legs, and there was blood, plenty of blood, all from under her dirty yellow dress. Her eyes were wide with terror and shock. I just froze as Miss Nelson's face went red.

"Miss Nelson, I'm bleeding . . ."

There was blood all over Lottie's legs and starting to drip beneath her chair on the floor. I felt myself shuddering as Miss Nelson led Lottie out of class and down to the nurse, I guess. "You'll be all right . . ." we heard Miss Nelson whispering.

No one in class said anything, no one but Dan Gooseherst, this fat round-headed kid who sat behind me, you know the one, with the red crew cut and freckles, the kid who had been held back from the sixth grade. He was awful mean most of the time because of it. He sat behind me grinning and laughing, making a big horse face.

"She got her period," he whispered too loud. "She didn't even know."

My mouth felt dry and hard.

They sent in Bucko, the grade school janitor, this guy in flannel with a bright red face, who used to drink from a tiny green bottle behind the dumpster in back of the building. The janitor mopped up the mess and disappeared back into the hall. Some of the boys began to laugh and make jokes. The girls in class were making faces at each other. I didn't know what to think. I mean, how was I supposed to know about any of this? No one had ever mentioned it. They never showed a girl getting her period on TV; hell, my brother sure never talked about it. Dan Gooseherst kept laughing and pointing, with the other boys joining in.

I guess then it hit me. No one had told poor Lottie. Who was going to tell her? Her old man? Her dumb older sister? She didn't ever seem to speak of a mother. The rest of the girls in class and the teachers sure didn't talk to her much. I looked around the room, listening to the other kids whispering and giggling, as Miss Nelson reappeared with Lottie. The poor girl went and got her jacket and book bag from the back of the room. Her dirty yellow dress was all stained with blood. Everyone was quiet. The room smelled like disinfectant now; its odor made me want to vomit.

As Lottie was walking out, Dan Gooseherst, from the seat behind me, whispered something to Bunny Rayburn beside him, and then laughed, just once. Lottie's face went white. I felt a knot turn in my gut. Miss Nelson's face froze. Her thin eyebrows snapped in place as she turned and faced the class.

"Who did that?" the teacher asked. "Who's laughing?"

No one offered a breath. You could hear Ralph the asthmatic, in the back of class, fighting to breathe.

"I said, who just laughed?"

Miss Nelson's fist snapped against her desk. Her eyes were black. "I want to know who was laughing right now or everyone's staying after school."

Dan Gooseherst raised his hand. I couldn't believe it. That loudmouth was going to turn himself in. I kind of shrugged my shoulders. Miss Nelson stared at Dan.

"Dan?"

"Dough Lunt, ma'am."

I turned and stared him right in the face.

"You're a goddamn liar . . ." I muttered.

"Dough!"

"Take it back . . ." I grunted.

"I can't. You did it," Dan said with a smile.

Miss Nelson stood right over me. I could feel the heat of her shadow boiling against my skin. I could feel the whole room swelling with silent stares. I looked Dan Gooseherst right in his eyes, then around the room, searching for some sort of glimmer of honesty, for something, but there was nothing, all their eyes were black as coal.

"You will both stay after school."

"But I didn't . . ." I mumbled.

"Not another word, Dough. Lottie, get your things, your sister will be here soon."

Miss Nelson led Lottie out of class once more as Dan Gooseherst smacked me in the back of the head. The rest of the day was a gray blur, until everyone else got to go home, everyone but me and Dan. Miss Nelson sat us down in front of her desk and lectured us for about a half hour about things I don't now remember and sure as heck didn't understand. All I knew was that I hadn't done a goddamn thing and Dan Gooseherst was going to get his house lit on fire. I would get my brother to help me take care of that.

"Do you understand?" was how Miss Nelson ended the lecture. We both nodded and put on our coats and stepped out into the playground to walk home. Once we were a block away from school, he grabbed me by my coat and said, "I'm gonna kick your ass for telling on me," and then he shoved me against a tree.

I pulled free, pushing him back. He was about my height but a lot heavier. He shoved me again and I smacked him on the side of his head with my fist.

"Let go, fat-ass," I said.

"Homo."

The gray sky loomed over us as we traded blows, walking down the block. At the corner, I knocked him into a bush and smiled. He sank into the green shrub, stuck, his legs and arms kind of wavering over his round body like an overturned bug. Then he pulled himself to his feet and chased after me. I started running toward the fields, hoping to lose him in the high grass, then stopped. Lottie, in her blue winter coat, was sitting up in a tree. For a moment, I thought she must have been a ghost. Then I saw that she had a handful of stones in her arms, and she started tossing them down at me, the first one hitting me right on the chin, the second one bouncing off my temple. I fell on my face as the whole world turned upside down. I laid on my side, covering my head, looking up into the sky as Lottie hurled a flat gray stone against the top of Dan's head, then a second, then a third.

"But he—" Dan tried to shout, but Lottie caught him on the forehead. Another stone hit his ear and then it started to bleed. From where I was laying, I noticed that Lottie was up there crying, she was shouting something, screaming in some undecipherable language, a stutter of cries and mumbles and hisses unrecognizable to the human ear, but I had heard it all before, I had spoken it, the cry of the defeated, the speech of the humiliated, the sound you make when your older brother sits on your chest and makes you hit yourself with your own hands. It was a sound I could recognize for sure. I got myself to my feet and started running away. I turned back once and saw she was still crying. Dan Gooseherst had managed to run back toward the school. He fell down a few feet away, then got up again and limped toward his home. I stopped running and crouched in the high prairie grass, holding my hand over the sore spot on my head, trying to breathe as quiet as I could.

I watched Lottie climb down out of the tree. She had her hood up and ran through the grass, still crying to herself. I waited until I was sure she was gone, then poked my head up and hurried down toward the culvert that led back toward the trailer park. I ran as fast as I could along the ditch until I saw something a few yards ahead. Kneeling down beside an irrigation pipe was Lottie, still whispering to herself, poking at the ground with a sharp stick. It must have been one of her hiding spots; there were old calendars with pictures of animals, tin cans, bottles with paper doll clothes pasted on them, and a few old suitcases filled with rocks. She looked up at me and I froze in my tracks.

"You're not my friend!" she shouted, her face creasing with tears. "You're not my friend at all." And then she crawled out of the ditch and ran off. I watched to be sure she was gone and then stared at the little fort she had made beside the irrigation pipe. There were a few detached doll heads and a little toy bunny in a pink dress. There were a few miniature tea cups wedged under the pipe. When I held one of the little tea cups in my hand, I got the feeling it was something that was supposed to be a secret, so I placed it back inside the pipe and headed toward home; as I hurried along the ditch, my eye felt sore and raw. I don't know why but I felt some tears moving down my face, burning along the open cut on my chin. I heard things moving in the high grass all around me; I heard things moving in the dark and held my breath until I got up the front stairs, because I was pretty certain that if I breathed once, I'd be dead.

dark eye of a dog

I don't know why but we were in love with death: On our homework, we drew pictures of the Devil disemboweling corpses with his impossibly large fangs. We collected pocket knives. We bleached animal skulls we found. We wore shark teeth on fake gold necklaces which we ordered from the back of comic books. We watched motorcross in hopes that something would go wrong, praying to witness someone's fiery ghost rising from the twisted wreckage below. We watched the *Faces of Death* videos whenever we were left alone. Somehow we understood that the world was a place of unquestionable brutality. Maybe we were looking for clues about our own father's death in every fly we dismembered. Maybe we hoped that if we came to some understanding of it, we would become immortal, or at least able to change our circumstances. We wanted to be like stuntmen. Or barbarians. We did not want to be afraid anymore, of anything, even the possibility of dying, so we did all we could to become accustomed to death.

One night, French took a seat beside my brother and me in front of the TV and asked what we thought about going with him to a dog fight. He looked around to be sure my mother was busy in the kitchen. "Well, what do you think?" He talked low as my mother clanged some dishes together, preparing dinner, opening and closing the rusty stove. It wasn't that French was a bad guy, because he really wasn't. I mean, he never beat on me or Pill or hit my mother, he never came home drunk and knocked a kitchen

50

joe meno

table over or threatened to kick our heads in for being unruly, but maybe that made it harder to get along with him. Somehow my mother had fallen for him and somehow he had convinced her to uproot us and sell our house and buy a trailer and move. But there was absolutely no way you could hate him for it. We had been living with him for a little less than a month already and he was still real nice and quiet and never raised his voice at anyone, even when he probably should have. He was still sweet with my mother and always offered to take us all out to dinner at the Sizzler in Aubrey. If he was watching a football or baseball game on Saturday afternoon and you said you wanted to watch a kung fu movie or the Saturday Horror Spectacular, he would take a swig of beer from its cold silver can and nod and watch the goddamn movie with you. My own old man would have laughed right in your face if you ever tried pulling a stunt like that. He would have laughed so hard you would have wondered what you were thinking to ask to change the channel in the first place. French, he never made you feel like that. He was soft-spoken and calm all the goddamn time. The only thing he did that was mildly irritating was urinate real loud at about 6 in the morning when he got up to go to work. Heck, our room was right next to the bathroom and he'd be in there every morning, just urinating for what seemed like hours. But that was about it. He was quiet as hell the rest of the time and always well-mannered. Nothing me or my crazy brother did could get a rise out of him. Maybe that's what burned us the most about him.

"Well, what do you think about coming with?" French muttered.

Me and my brother sat on either side of him, staring at the blue-and-white flicker of the television screen.

"What?" I asked. "Mom doesn't know, does she?"

My mother ran a spoon through a bowl, mixing up another one of her ungodly casseroles. She could take any three good ingredients and make a horrible mess out of it. Any of the meat French brought home from the plant, secondhand meat products that he got real cheap, would turn to unrecognizable things in my mother's hands. Take three foods you think you like, something simple like turkey, noodles, and celery, right? My mother could mix those things up in a way that would make you wonder what exactly happened from the time she put it all in a pan and put it in the oven and then put it on your plate. I could hear the stove whine as my mother opened the oven door and popped the poor casserole inside.

French shook his head slowly. He had a long pale face with deep blue eyes. His hair was brown and thinning and he wore it short in a crew cut that showed the shine of the side of his head right above his pointy ears. "Do you think I'm plum crazy? Of course your mother doesn't know." His eyes sparkled behind his brown-rimmed glasses like magic.

I smiled, nodding like a maniac. "Sure. I'll go." A dog fight. A goddamn dog fight. I'd never been to anything like that before. The closest I'd ever been was when the Dilforts' big black labrador got loose and killed Gretchen Hollis's four white kittens back in Duluth. The dog snapped their necks and left them in a single pool of dark red blood beside the Hollises' house. The Hollises were so upset that they planted four white wood crosses in the meadow beside their house in memory of the dead kittens and all. That spot was a perfect place to go and smoke a cigarette or stare at a nudie magazine, because it was dark and shady and all the little kids in the neighborhood thought the place was haunted.

"What about you, Pill?" French whispered. "You in?"

Pill shrugged his shoulders.

"I don't care."

"Well, do you want to go or not, pal?" French asked with a smile. He pushed his glasses tight against his nose.

"Sure. Whatever. I don't care."

Apathy was the only thing my older brother seemed to know those days. I just hoped that sooner or later he'd go back to being how he had been in Duluth.

"All right then. We'll leave right after dinner. Not a word to your mother now, understand?"

I nodded excitedly. Pill shrugged his shoulders and continued staring at the television screen.

"Now go help her set the table," French whispered, taking another slug of his beer. I shot off the couch like a rocket and pulled the dinner plates from the cabinet. My brother just sighed and took his seat at the table. French flipped off the TV and followed. My mother pulled the casserole out of the oven, placed it in the center of the little round wood table, right on top of the checkered yellow tablecloth, and everyone sucked in their breath.

"Looks great," I lied, folding my napkin into the collar of my shirt the way my old man used to. My mother smiled and spooned a big helping on to my plate. It steamed and congealed and oozed mysteriously, but I didn't falter. I closed my eyes and began to force it down with a fake smile across my face. Pill just poked at his food, mixing it up with his fork, pushing it back and forth. His technique was to spread the poor food all across his plate in a flat plane of creamy ooze so it appeared like he had eaten most of it, but no parent I ever knew was fooled by that trick, so he took a bite and shuddered, spitting it into his napkin for cover.

"This is great, honey," French mumbled across the yellow table. "Clean your plates, boys, so we can take off."

"Take off? Where are you all heading?" my mother asked, wiping her lips with the edge of her napkin.

"Well, we were all gonna head over to Aubrey and pick up some parts for the Impala." French smiled, scraping a fork over his plate. A lie. Ol' French was lying right to my mother's face. Maybe this guy wasn't as perfect as he seemed. He shoved another forkful of yellowed noodles into his mouth and forced it down. "Mmmm," he said with a smile. "Great."

Pill rolled his eyes and spat another mouthful of food into his napkin, folded it up under the table, and forced it into his front pocket. The horrible glob on his plate was not disappearing. It seemed to be growing, actually, bubbling a little, expanding across his plate. He grunted to himself, shaking his head in frustration. Me, I wasn't fairing any better. What was left of the horrible casserole had dried up and become a thick substance that felt awful against my gums. I swallowed, nearly gagging, and started to cough. French shook his head, wiping his mouth on his napkin.

"All right, boys, let's go." French crossed his fork and knife over his plate and pushed his chair away from the table.

"But they're not even done eating," my mom said with a frown.

"Oh, they're fine." French smiled, kissing my mother on her forehead. "Besides, we want to make sure we get there before the store closes."

French winked at me and I nodded back. This guy couldn't be all that bad.

We piled into my mother's rusted-out Corolla and drove out to the barn where the dog fight would be taking place. French had met some guy while he was drinking at the bowling alley a few nights before and he told French all about it. Nearly every man in town would be there. No women, no girls. They were pitting Lester Deegan's young shepherd against Stu Freeman's old pit bull. I guess the way they did it was they'd beat on the poor dogs, riling them up with rods and broom handles, and then turn the two animals loose on each other. The barn was off Mill Creek Road, way out of town, in the gray brush behind someone's ranch. The barn was shiny and red like it had just been painted. There was a line of cars, mostly pickups and big Chevys with V-8s, some stock GMs, all parked one beside another. There was some yellow light breaking between the panels in the barn walls. "This is it." French patted me on the head. He turned off my mother's Corolla and hopped out of the car. The autumn air was cool around us as me and Pill followed French toward the barn.

"Hey there, French, glad you could make it," some guy with a red mustache said, smiling as we walked through the side door. French: I was surprised that some guy knew his name. Maybe they worked at the plant together. Heck, I guess French was a supervisor. People were bound to know him around town. We stepped inside and the glare of the big yellow lights made me squint.

Nearly every man in Tenderloin was packed into this barn. Thick plumes of cigar and cigarette smoke drifted in the air under the bright lights. There were old men with pale gray faces and white cowboy hats sitting on stools in the back and younger boys with mussed brown hair running around, pushing each other into the dirt. There were middle-aged men in their coveralls and work clothes passing around silver flasks of booze. There were big-shouldered teenagers spitting tobacco into the gray dust with conviction, while me and my brother followed French, edging our way toward the middle of the crowd.

In the center of the barn was a ring. It was a small section of about ten feet rounded out by some chicken wire about five feet high. There were breaks in the fence at opposite ends where some crude gates had been built. French patted me on the shoulder and pointed across the ring. "There's Lester Deegan's dog," he whispered. The dog was big, a brown and black German shepherd with a long, thick snout. Its eyes were nearly green and its gums were pinkish with blood. Its tongue flagged in and out of its red metal muzzle, which kept its jaws closed tight.

"That's the champeen," this kid, Billy Pillick, mumbled, elbowing me in the side. Billy was a year younger than me but twice my size. He had a pug nose and it seemed like most of his teeth were missing. He was always getting in trouble at school for eating some other kid's lunch. I would see him on the playground at recess, putting other kids in headlocks. The dog's owner, Mr. Deegan, had a brown hunting jacket on and his face was shadowed by a white cowboy hat. He held his dog on a leather leash, keeping him close, right outside one of the gates. Mr. Deegan looked like he was more intelligent than the rest of the men there. He was the local livestock veterinarian and I kind of wondered why he'd put his dog through such a thing. His face was stern and serious, his mouth tight-lipped. His dog, the shepherd, had the same quiet calm, the same stern look in the black of its eyes.

Mr. Deegan led the shepherd, Lance, by the leash into the rounded metal ring, tying the dog to a metal hook, still looking calm and resigned the whole way. There, on the other side of the pen, was the challenger, a pit bull. This dog was pale, blue-white almost, pink-nosed with silvery trails of drool that ran from its muzzle. There were pink scars all along its body. This white dog was huge. Nearly twice the size of the other poor dog. It kept snorting out loads of drool from its square jaws, flicking its triangular ears as some flies swarming around its head. This dog was going to tear that other dog to pieces. It kept yanking on the metal leash, trying to get free, rearing up on its big square paws.

Mr. Freeman, the pit bull's owner, yanked the metal chain, leading it through the gate. He wore a red hunting cap with the furry bill nearly covering his red eyes. His face was dark and whiskered. He sold propane and rented moving vehicles. I guess he had fallen off a thresher when he was a kid and had lost a foot to the awful machine, so now he walked with a limp, shifting his weight to one side of his body, then back, limping along with his huge white dog. The pit bull suddenly reared up on its hind legs, tearing at the wire fence with its enormous paws.

"Down!" Mr. Freeman yelled. "Down, you mangy mutt!" Mr. Freeman's face was red and pock-marked. A sheen of sweat had begun to form along his forehead.

I looked over and saw French as he pulled a plug of tobacco from inside his jacket, then cut a nice piece of chaw from its slick black mass and planted it in my hand. Heck, I had never even seen the man spit tobacco before in my life. He didn't say a word either, just handed me some and stared across the ring at the brown shepherd, Lance, like he had handed me tobacco a hundred times before.

"Do you want some there, Pill?" French asked, cutting another piece loose. Pill shook his head. He was about as friendly as a goddamn tick. It was beginning to make me angry. Here French was, going out of his way to try to be nice, offering us chaw like our own old man might have, and Pill was being a dickwad about it all. French just sunk the chaw between his gums and cheek and put the plug back in his jacket. He leaned in close and whispered, "Don't swallow any of that spit now or you'll get a sore stomach."

I nodded, watching how French had placed the chaw in his mouth. I slipped the tobacco between my bottom lip and gum. It tasted sweet like molasses and began to liquefy, bleeding syrup down the back of my throat. I gagged a little.

"Spit," French said, smiling out of the corner of his mouth. I nodded and spat a load of slick brown juice like a pro, watching it plop in the dust. My face felt good because I was smiling. I felt like a man all right, spitting tobacco and watching these other men swear and swig from the passing flask of whiskey. French winked and patted me on the back.

"Who do you boys favor?" he asked.

I shrugged my shoulders, spitting again. "I like that shepherd."

"Yeah? That pit bull looks awfully mean," French said.

"That other dog's gonna tear that shepherd in two," Pill muttered.

"We'll see," I mumbled, leaning against the wire fence. I looked around the ring again. The pit bull was growling and snarling and drooling as Mr. Freeman jabbed it in the side with the end of a broom handle. The dog yelped and snapped at the handle, unable to open its jaws on account of the silver muzzle. Mr. Freeman jabbed at the dog again. The other dog stood at the opposite end of the ring, scratching in the dust as it flicked its ears.

After some time, they turned those poor dogs loose.

My dog, the shepherd, Lance, was awful quiet. It hadn't even begun snarling, even when its owner began riling it up, jabbing its flanks with the end of a stick. Mr. Deegan pulled the red muzzle off and untied the leash, then hopped out of the ring. I felt like closing my eyes right then. That poor dog was going to be ripped apart.

The pit bull was snarling and spitting and nearly ready to climb up over the wire fence. Mr. Freeman yanked the muzzle and leash free, then hurried through the opening in the gate.

My dog was as good as doomed. There was a single moment when all the men got quiet and it seemed like even the dogs were silent, right when those two animals first locked eyes, when they first saw each other beneath those shiny yellow lights. A single drop of sweat fell from my forehead and made me feel like dying.

My dog lunged forward, not making a sound. Its clean jaws bit down on the pit bull's front right paw, clamping it right at the joint, tearing and drooling spit and dark red blood. The pit bull just sat there for a moment. Then the dog tried to yank its paw free, not snarling or biting back; it yelped a little and tried to pull away. Blood broke out along the white dog's flesh, spilling along the gray dirt in perfectly round dollops.

"Kill! Shilo, kill!" Mr. Freeman yelled, shaking the wire fence. But his dog wouldn't move. It snarled a little, as good old Lance snapped at the bloody front paw again, clamping down hard once more and snarling. The shepherd shook its head wildly, tearing the other dog's front paw from its joint.

"Je-sus!!" someone shouted. I couldn't move. I couldn't look away. I clenched the wire fence and held my breath as more blood darkened the dirt around the white dog's flanks.

"Kill!" Mr. Freeman shouted. "Shilo, kill, you lousy mutt!"

There was a milky-white silence in the pitt bull's pink eyes. The shepherd growled, going for the pit bull's throat now.

"Kill, Shilo, kill!"

Suddenly the white dog snapped awake; its black eyes darkened as it bled from its missing paw. It snarled and lunged, clamping some fur around the shepherd's neck, tearing it loose with one huge swipe.

"No!" I shouted. The shepherd pulled itself free and backed away a little, circling as it moved. The dust in the air began to cloud my eyes and throat. I felt like I couldn't hardly breathe at all. Tiny droplets of blood broke from the shepherd's bare neck. The torn fur there was dark and shiny. Blood gathered in a clot at the base of its neck.

"Kill! Shilo, kill!" Mr. Freeman shouted again, shaking the fence. The shepherd's owner, Mr. Deegan, was silent. He stood straight-faced and stern at the opposite side of the ring, holding the wire fence.

The pit bull and shepherd were circling each other. Their teeth were full of blood and spit. Their eyes were black, blacker than black, almost empty. They moved close to the dirty ground, tensed and mean and snarling. I looked up and saw my older brother gripping the wire fence too. His face was pale. His eyes were bright and fixed as he mumbled something to himself like a prayer. French's face was the same way, all tensed and staring straight ahead, as the dogs stopped circling and locked eyes once more.

"Kill!"

The dust and smoke in the barn seemed to rise. That voice rang out loud and clear and I thought it was Mr. Freeman again, but it wasn't, it was sharp and stern and orderly—Mr. Deegan was shouting now. His face was solemn as he let out the command. His shepherd obeyed, lunging forward, catching its teeth on the side of the pit bull's short white face, digging its incisors square through the flesh and into the dog's dark black eye.

"Goddamn!" the man beside me shouted, peeking through his folded hand.

The pit bull howled, rolling into the dirt, as the shepherd bit down hard on the other dog's muzzle, tearing the eye from its socket in a mess of thick blood. I squinted, shaking my head, and French squeezed my shoulder. French's face was all tensed around his eyes, like he was having problems stomaching it all. But my brother didn't move. He just stared ahead, dumbfounded, I guess, holding the fence tight as it held him up too.

"No!" Mr. Freeman shouted, tossing his red hunting cap to the dirt by his feet. "No!"

The pit bull rolled in the dirt, clawing at its empty eye socket. The eye had disappeared in the blood and dirt and mud, as the shepherd lunged again, gripping the soft fleshy meat under the pit bull's throat. It dug its teeth into the skin, pulling a clump of fur and flesh free, snarling in the blood and drool as the big white pit bull laid on its side, still and as good as dead.

My mouth was dry. My heart was pounding in my chest so hard that I could feel my blood beating in my ears. The shepherd sniffed around the other animal a few times, then lifted its ears, confused, whining a little. Mr. Deegan clapped his hands and the shepherd bolted back to him. Carefully, he fit the muzzle over the shepherd's jaws, opening a black valise to tend to its wounds. French let out a low whistle, shaking his head slowly.

My brother's face was bright red. His knuckles were cold and white as he still gripped the fence. "Now what?!" he shouted at French.

French took a deep breath, shrugging his shoulders a little.

"Now I guess they shoot the poor thing."

My brother turned back to face the ring.

"They can't shoot that thing," Pill muttered. French laid his hand on my brother's shoulder. Some of the men milled around, settling bets, trading soft wads of cash from hand to hand, smiling and spitting in the dirt. Other men just stood there, sharing sips from a bottle or a flask. The barn began to empty out. Slowly, the stink of cigars and the gray cloud of dust settled around us as my brother held the fence, shaking his head.

"C'mon, boys, we better get on home. Your mother probably already called the state police on us." French patted my head and smiled. My brother didn't move.

"Let's go, Pill, 'fore it gets too late."

The pit bull laid in the dirt, its thick white sides still rising and falling.

"This is it?" Pill muttered. "This is it?" His eyes were red like he was about to cry. He kept holding the fence, gritting his teeth to keep the tears down inside. I knew exactly how he felt. I wished I had never seen it; I wished we had never come. French stood still and stared at my brother's face without saying a word, then walked slowly toward the center of the ring, where the white dog was whining. Pill and I followed, unsure of what to say or do. Mr. Freeman was standing over his poor animal, and Mr. Deegan stared at it sadly too.

"Whatever you want to do," Mr. Freeman was saying. He

handed a huge fold of cash to Mr. Deegan. "I mean, it's your dog now. You want me to shoot it?"

Mr. Deegan stared down at the white dog. "Let's have a look." He squatted beside the dog's square head, then ran his palm over its side.

"Didn't fight very well, did it?" Mr. Deegan asked with a frown.

"No, it did not, and I wouldn't like talking about it now if you don't mind."

"I could patch up his eye and paw and neck all right, but I'm just wondering if it's worth it."

"I'd just the same shoot it as waste the time," Mr. Freeman grunted, digging his hands into his pants pockets. Mr. Deegan stood and stared down at the dog and shrugged his shoulders.

French glanced down at me, then my brother, and frowned. "Go ahead and wait in the car. I need to talk to someone from the plant." He raised his voice just a little, staring down into the dirt. "Go on," he repeated when we didn't move, and he began to walk toward Mr. Deegan.

I pulled on my brother's shirt. He shook his head, cussed a little, then turned and headed out of the barn. I followed, not saying a word, just watching how he kicked the dirt with his shoes, then punched the side of my mother's rusted-out car. The line of big trucks and stock cars began to file out, their headlights flashing on, then their engines, before disappearing into the dark. The night sky hung right over our heads, lit up with the stars and the moon. The air was cool and dusty and blew against our backs. Pill-Bug punched the car once more and stared back at the barn.

"I hate him," he muttered, digging his fists into his pockets. "I do. Thinks he can tell me what to do. I'll cut his throat in his sleep."

The red barn door swung open after a few minutes and

French and Mr. Deegan stepped out, carrying something between the two of them. They walked up to us and the car, kicking up dust, as the broken light from the stars and the barn flashed across our faces.

There was the pit bull, all bandaged up and quiet, wrapped in a thin blue blanket, resting in their arms.

"Don't say a word," French mumbled, breathing hard.

My brother shook his head. His face went all red and tense. "What the hell's that?"

"I said, don't say a word." French frowned, unlocking the blue hatchback. Mr. Deegan and French gently slid the big white dog inside.

"You can't bring that on home," Pill muttered. "What are you doing?"

"Keep quiet," French whispered, slowly closing the hatchback. French wiped some sweat from his forehead and dug in his back pocket. He pulled out his brown leather wallet, the same wallet me and my older brother had stolen from so many times, and fished out two crisp twenty-dollar bills and planted them in Mr. Deegan's soft white palm.

"There you go, Mr. Deegan." French smiled, shoving his wallet into his back pocket. Mr. Deegan shook his head, folding the cash up. He looked down through the back window at the slumbering animal inside.

"Now, I can't guarantee that that animal will live for long," he said. "He's on a sedative right now, so he should be all right for the night. But if he gets wild on you or you notice the wounds not healing right, give me a call. You should bring him by the office in the next few days and I'll change the dressing and give you some more medication."

French nodded and shook hands with him.

My older brother was dumbfounded. I couldn't help smiling,

shaking my head at the crazy thought of it all, grinning as we piled into the blue car.

"Mom's never gonna stand for it," Pill grunted, slamming the car door shut.

"She will if we tell her we found the dog on the side of the road and we brought it home to keep it from dying all alone out there."

"She ain't ever gonna believe that." Pill stared straight ahead with a mean, sour look, crossing his arms across his chest. "Who asked you to get that damn dog anyway?"

"No one. I did it for myself. I need a bird dog for the winter."

"Bird dog? That ain't a bird dog. That dog can't even see. It's missing a goddamn eye. I ain't gonna lie to my mother."

"Enough already. You tell your mother what you want, Pill. I ain't asking you to lie to her. But on account of that poor animal lying back there, you might just wanna keep your mouth shut so as not to ruin our chances here."

He sounded like one of us now. He stared at the open black road, gripping the wheel tightly. He checked in the rearview mirror every couple of seconds, watching as the dark blue blanket rose and fell with the dog's breath.

Before long, we were home, and Pill shot out of the car and into the trailer before the car's engine even died.

"Give me a hand with him, pal?" French asked, unlocking the hatchback. The door rose and squeaked as French leaned over and rubbed the dog's side.

"How come you did it, French?" I asked, peering up into his long white face. He rubbed the sweat between his glasses and the bridge of his nose and then let out a sigh.

"I don't know, kiddo, I thought it was the right thing to do. Your brother's been in a kinda mood since we moved here and he seemed pretty upset by that dog getting hurt, and so I thought maybe I could, you know, make him feel better about things, but I guess it didn't work out so well, huh?"

"Guess not."

"Can't get rid of the poor thing now, can we?" He seemed to answer himself with a shrug of his shoulders. "You gonna stick to the story?" he asked, leaning over the car. His face was shiny with sweat and his eyes were dark behind his glasses.

"I guess so. Long as I don't get in trouble for lying."

"You won't. Here, now give his legs a little lift."

I dug my hands under the blue blanket. The dog stirred a little as we made our way up the front steps. The screen door clanged open and my mother shot up from the couch, raising her thin black eyebrows.

"What is this?" she asked, covering her mouth in surprise. French and I laid the dog down on the sofa and frowned.

"Found him . . . on the side of the road," French grunted. "Brought him to Mr. Deegan." French couldn't even look at my mother as he lied. He just stared down at the animal as it dug its face into the cushions of the couch. Pill was nowhere to be found. He had gone off to our bedroom to pout.

"But why didn't you leave it with Mr. Deegan?" my mother asked.

"Oh, he was gonna put it to sleep and the boys took a liking to it so . . ."

"It's huge," my mother said. "See how big its paw is? We can't keep that thing in here." Her eyes went big as she looked over the animal's body. "What happened to its eye? Oh, and its other paw."

"Must've been hit by a car or something," French replied. He stared at me and gave a little nod with his head.

"Can we keep it, Mom?" I asked on cue. "It won't bother no one, I promise. And I'll take care of it. Pill will help too."

"I don't know," she whispered, staring at the pit bull's square jaws. She bit her bottom lip, thinking hard. "Where's it gonna sleep?"

"It can sleep out here," I answered.

"What about shots and rabies and all that?"

"We got that taken care of," French said.

"I dunno . . ."

"Thanks, Mom!" I gave her a good hug around her waist and stared down at that big white dog. It laid still, wrapped in the blue blanket, burying its face back under the sofa cushions. I glanced up at French and nodded. He was smiling nervously, running his hand along the dog's side, patting it gently. I guess right then I started to wonder how much longer he'd stick around before he finally had enough of us all—between my mother, who was prone to fits of crying in the middle of the night, and me and my brother running wild all around the goddamn trailer park. I stared at his long white face and nodded to myself. Sure, one morning we'd wake up and French would be gone, maybe the big black Impala would still be on the blocks out front, maybe some of his clothes would still be in my mother's closet, but like all the men in my mother's life, he would disappear without a right word or reason. Maybe my mother would pack up all of his things in a brown cardboard box and send it off to him, maybe he'd come by the trailer to pick it up when no one was around, but eventually he'd be gone and less than a blurry photo in my own mind. I thought I could be decent to him until then, because I knew it wouldn't be very long.

The big dog rolled on its other side, yelping a little.

"Somebody should stay out here with it tonight," French offered, rubbing its soft fur with his fingers. I nodded, stroking its white belly.

"Well, you've got school tomorrow, pal," my mother said with a frown in my direction.

"I'll do it, I guess," French mumbled.

"Did you guys already come up with a name for it?" my mother asked.

"Shilo," French said with a nod.

"Shilo? What kind of name is that?" She smiled, rubbing its side. "What about Spot or Pluto or something nice like that?"

"No, Shilo's good," I said, nodding too.

"All right then, I better pick up some dog food on the way home from work," my mother said. She rubbed the dog's sore white belly. "Good grief. Looks like it's some kind of monster."

After that, the dumb dog became the biggest baby I'd ever seen. My mother didn't seem to pay too much attention to it during the first few weeks; but she ended up being the one who fed it every day and gave it its medicine. After a while, it seemed like the dog had always been there, like it was just one other dirty mouth to feed. The dog would just lie around with its ugly head drooling in your lap as you watched TV, or it would beg for scraps at the table, staring at you with the poorest single black eye you'd ever seen. Once all its wounds healed, its empty eye was a hard gray-and-black cavern that had to be sealed up with stitches. Its one leg that had lost a paw became hard and black too, a thick bumpy wound that ended just below its joint. Its neck healed fine, but left three or four huge pink scars. That dog would hop around on its three legs and rub its muzzle against your thigh or leap up and lick your face or come and lay right on top of you.

French was the worst for babying it; the two of them would just sit on the couch for hours. French would let the animal take licks from his beer can and rub its ugly one-eyed face in front of the TV. Of course, if the dog knocked over one of my mother's flowerpots or ate a whole plate of fried chicken, French would holler, "Dough, take care of your dog here." I guess Pill and that dog never much got along. Maybe it had been like the whole world had let him down again when Shilo lost that fight. Once, I saw my brother give that dog a kick, and because of its missing paw, it rolled right onto its side, but that's all it did, just laid there like it had wanted to rest right there in that exact spot in the first place. Me, I tried like hell to take care of that miserable animal, but it had been an old dog to begin with and wouldn't run or fetch or roll over or do any dog trick you could think of except sic, which didn't do much good, because that damn dog couldn't move after *anything* fast enough to catch it. So the dog would end up clamping its teeth down on your pant leg or shirttail and would refuse to let go until it got tired of playing or tore a hole in your clothes or until you finally gave in and took off your shirt and left it your clothes to chew on. It was a good dog, but for a ten-year-old, not much fun to play with. I guess I got used to taking it out for a walk twice a day in the field behind the trailer park so it could do its business. I'd watch it hop on home and return to its couch to watch whatever was on television, sitting there beside the rest of us.

At night it would crowd me in my own bed. I would never admit it, but I was happy when it did that. Its awful breath would be warm against my face. Its white muzzle would be buried beneath the blankets beside my neck, snoring loudly. I would lie there and stare up at the strange shapes of the wood grain of the top bunk above my head, seeing in the dark rounded lines only skulls and Devil faces and knives, images from slasher movies my brother had forced me to watch, afraid to admit I was scared of the dark. I would lie there, wishing Pill had said goodnight to me or that there was a nightlight of some kind. The sounds of the trailer would echo like fangs in the darkness. I would lie there, secretly happy that Shilo was the last thing I would see before I fell asleep. The footsteps of the slashers suddenly fell away. I would stop worrying that a ghost was going to come in and cut my throat.

the devil in his place

Almost every day for a week, Lottie, that loony girl, followed me home from school. I couldn't understand why she thought we were friends again. I would glance over my shoulder and try to ignore her, but she'd always be behind me, singing to herself, skipping along the culvert. She would try to talk to me, hurrying to catch, up, talking all kinds of nonsense, like how her old man had cut his thumb off and ran two miles to get it sewn back on. I did not like her and I tried to make that clear.

One Wednesday afternoon after school, I was watching cartoons on TV, enjoying having the sofa to myself, when I heard a knock at the screen door, and there she was, waving at me. What she asked me just then made about as much sense as anything else she ever said: "Do you wanna go see the hanging ghost?"

"What?" I muttered, not stepping too close to the door. Like always, her hair was twisted up in four or five pigtails, pulling her pale skin taut around her eyebrows. She had on a dirty gray dress and big brown boots that must have belonged to her older brother.

"Do you wanna go to the Furnhams' farm? It's not too far a walk from here." She was picking something from her tiny ear and staring back at me with her small, brownish-gray eyes.

"What the hell are doing at my house?" I said quietly so my mother in the kitchen couldn't hear.

Lottie shrugged her shoulders, still picking at her ear. "They got a dead horse out there. That's where Mr. Furnham hung himself. Right out in the barn."

I thought for sure this girl, Lottie, was nuts. Shilo sniffed around the door, rubbing its pink nose against the screen. *Kill*, I wanted to say. *Sic.* But I didn't. I just stared at her round face, looking at the way her eyes never remained still in her head.

"Well, do ya?" she asked again.

I stepped back from the screen, itching my eyes like they hurt. A week before, this girl had thrown stones at me, and now she wanted me to go to some barn with her. I didn't know what to say that would clue her in to how I did not want anything to do with her.

"There really are ghosts out there," she whispered.

I shook my head and decided to lie.

"I gotta eat soon," I mumbled. It was only 4:30 in the afternoon. My mother was in the kitchen defrosting a leg of lamb that wouldn't be ready for another few hours. "Sorry." I tried to smile but Lottie poked her head right against the screen. Her little round nose had a gray ring of sweat underneath it. She smelled like a boy. My dumb dog sniffed the girl through the door and whined for her attention.

"Is that yours?" she asked.

"Yeah," I said, nodding.

"That's a pretty dog." Lottie smiled, rubbing her hand against the screen so my big dumb dog would lick her palm. "Sure is friendly."

"Sure, sure, whatever."

"So you're eatin' right now?" she asked.

"Yeah," I lied again, trying to back away from the door. "I just asked my mom. Sorry."

"Oh." Her eyes became small and sad. She moved away from the door as I breathed a breath of relief.

Of course, just then my mother's voice rose like song from the other room: "You have plenty of time to go out, Dough. Just be back by 6, okay?"

"But Mom, I—"

"No, no, you need to get out of this house and get some exercise. You don't wanna end up like Joe Landon, do you?"

Poor Joe Landon, one of our old neighbors back in Duluth, was infamous for never leaving his house. He was a couple of years older then me and my brother, a teenager, I guess. He had a huge white freckled face and a short red crew cut that showed his tiny, pointed ears. There were at least a million neighborhood kids on our block who played stickball or catch-one-catch-all, but this kid, Joe Landon, just stayed inside and ate and slept in front of the TV until he was nearly three hundred pounds and all pasty and white and his parents had to sell their house to put him in some special clinic somewhere in Minneapolis. Joe Landon was someone my mother was always warning me about.

"But Mom, I've got homework and—"

"You've got all night to do it. Stop being rude and go out and play."

I gritted my teeth, feeling humiliated.

"There really is a ghost out there," Lottie repeated with a smile, pressing against the screen door. I shook my head and pulled my dirty baseball hat down over my eyes. This was going to be worse than going to Sunday school. But I made a plan right there. Stay with her a little while, maybe walk down the long road toward all the farms, then ditch her and run home and make it back to the trailer to doze in front of the TV.

"You gonna come out then?" Lottie grinned.

"Yeah, yeah, hold on," I grunted. I stole one of my brother's shirts and checked to see if there were a couple crumpled-up cigarettes stashed inside one of the pockets. There were. Three lonely

squares. Enough for sure. I unlocked the screen and stepped outside. My dumb dog lapped at the door behind me. I hopped down
the gray cement steps and looked around. Most of the trailer park
was empty. Most everyone was still at work. There were some little kids running around half-naked, wearing only their diapers,
chasing each other in front of a trailer down by the end of the cul-
de-sac. There was a skinny mother in a long blue dress sitting on
her front porch, combing out her long yellow hair, watching her
little naked babies playing in the dirt. The sun was out. The sky
was pretty and blue and it was almost as hot as summer. I tightened my baseball cap right down around my eyes again. Lottie was
just standing there, staring at me. She was leaning beside the ugliest girl's bicycle, too small for her for sure, with pink streamers
hanging from the handlebars and silver noisemakers in the spokes.

"That your bike?" I asked.

"Yeah. It used to be my sister's. She's too old to ride now. You
can try it if you want."

"No, that's okay, I'll walk."

"You sure? It's a good bike."

"Yeah, I bet."

"Haw. Okay, then." Lottie shrugged her shoulders and took a
seat on her pink bike and began pedaling around me in wide circles as we started down the road toward the Furnhams' barn.

"You like living in a trailer park?" she asked, nearly cutting me
off as she finished a big figure-eight.

"No."

"How come?"

"Because it's stupid."

"Why?"

"Because it is, okay?"

"Okay."

She circled around me again on her crappy pink bike. Her

awkward knees hung out from under her dress as she pedaled. The
lousy noisemakers in the spokes sparkled as she rode. "Do you like
your name?" she asked.

I stopped walking and watched her wheel around. "Hey, listen,
I ain't gonna walk with you if you keep asking stupid questions." I
accentuated that with a good solid spit, then started walking again.
I fumbled through my brother's shirt pocket and put a cigarette in
my mouth, then took out a book of matches from my own pants
and lit the square, coughing a little as I inhaled.

"How come you smoke?" Lottie asked, swerving past me.

"What?"

"How come you smoke?" she repeated.

"Because I do. Jesus," I grunted.

"You do it 'cause you think it's cool." She smiled, shaking her
head. "You do it 'cause you think it makes you look older."

"Shut the hell up for a minute, will ya?" I inhaled and
coughed again.

"Haw! You don't even know how to do it right." She giggled,
shaking her pigtails behind her round head.

"Forget it!" I shouted, and stopped walking. "I'm going
home."

"No, no, don't go home," she pleaded. She stopped her bike
right in front of me. "I won't ask any more questions, honest.
Okay? I promise."

"How 'bout you don't speak at all?" I said, staring at her lousy
face. She smiled and began pedaling again. I started walking.

"Do you like Miss Nelson?" she asked. Miss Nelson. Oh, Miss
Nelson. Of course I liked Miss Nelson. I loved Miss Nelson. But we
had gotten off on the wrong foot and there was no going back now.

"No, I don't like Miss Nelson," I said with a frown.

"Oh, I thought you liked her. I thought you wanted to marry
her."

"You're crazy." I tried to smile, offering a phony chuckle. "You're nuts, that's what you are."

"I thought you wanted to marry her and run away with her."

"Did anyone ever tell you that you talk a lot?"

She stopped and shrugged her shoulders. "No."

I shook my head and kept walking, taking another drag on my cigarette.

"Do you like any girls in class?" she asked.

"What?"

"Do you like Mary Beth Clishim?" she said with a smile, winking at me a little.

"What?" I stared at her round face and gray eyes. "No, I don't like her."

"All the boys do." Her lips curled into a smirk.

"Well, I don't."

"Do you like Laurie Avers?"

"No." I swatted at a fly that buzzed past my head.

"What about Jill?"

"Jill who?"

"Jill Montefort. Do you like her?"

"No, already. Jesus, you don't ever shut up, do you?"

"What about Miss Nelson? You like her, don't you? You can tell me."

"You're giving me a goddamn headache."

"Well, you have to like somebody."

"Why's that?" I asked.

"Everyone likes somebody."

"No, not me. I don't like anybody. I don't like anybody anywhere." I flicked the dying cigarette to the side of the road.

"Haw. What about your brother? You like him?" This girl was trying to be real funny.

"What, are you queer? Course I don't like my brother."

"Haw. What about Texas? Do you like Texas?"

"God, you're loony."

"Sure, sure." She smiled, pedaling beside me. Her eyes were all bright and shiny, then she said it. "Do you like . . . me?"

I shrugged my shoulders, staring at my feet as I walked. "I like you about as much as that rock over there." I pointed to a round gray stone covered in green moss and grass.

"Is that a lot?" she asked with a frown.

"You figure it out."

"Oh, you don't have to be shy with me. My sister told me all about what boys think."

"How's that?"

She kept tilting her head back and forth like she was singing a song to herself as she spoke. "My sister told me that when a boy acts like he doesn't like you, it means he really does."

"She told you that?"

Lottie nodded proudly, giving me another gruesome wink.

"Well, your sister is wrong. I don't like you because I don't like you."

"Haw!" She smirked again and shook her head. "Are you a virgin?"

"Jesus!" I shouted, shaking my head. "What in the hell's wrong with you?"

"Are you?"

"Why the hell would I tell you about any of that stuff?"

This girl was truly nuts. She was giggling like crazy now, shaking her head and smiling to herself. "Did you ever have sex?" she asked in a whisper.

"Why the hell do wanna know so bad?"

"I don't think you did." Her gray teeth shone under her nose as she grinned. "Do you know how to have sex?" she whispered, stopping her bike in its tracks. Her face was all shiny with sweat.

One of her pigtails began to unravel on the side of her head.

"Yeah," I kind of mumbled, looking away from her.

"Really?"

"Yeah, already, I said I do!"

She stared at me hard, edging her teeth along her bottom lip. I tried to stare back, squinting a little. Right then, she had to know it was a lie. Her eyes were all sharp and mean and she smiled a little to herself. My face felt hot. The whole back of my neck felt like it was bubbling with sweat. I looked away and began walking again.

"I think you're lying. I don't think you know the first thing about doing it."

"So what? What the hell do you care?"

Lottie shrugged her shoulders and began pedaling again. She wouldn't stop grinning. Her eyes were nearly crossed from her smiling so hard. I rubbed the back of my neck and scratched my face.

"Where the hell is this place anyway?" I shouted, digging my hands in my pockets.

"Right there." She pointed to a huge red barn, worn and crooked, that stood a few hundred feet away, behind a low wire fence. The barn looked spooky as hell. Sunlight poured through the breaks in the roof in thick silver beams, cutting the dust in the air like the hand of God or something. There was an old red tractor parked beside it and a ways back from that was the Furnhams' white farmhouse, graying along the porch and roof.

"That's it, huh?" I mumbled.

"You scared?" Lottie smiled.

"No, I'm not scared."

Lottie set down her ugly bike in the long yellow grass beside the wire fence. Then she hopped over like a pro, landing on her feet with a little grunt. I followed, catching my left foot on a loose wire, tripping to my knees as I fell on the other side.

"There's their house," Lottie whispered, pointing to the white building as we walked up the path toward the barn. "And that's the barn. That's where he did it." She frowned. Her eyes were dark and shallow. Her whole face was gray.

"Did what?"

"Hung himself," she whispered again, staring straight at the huge red door. "His crops all died and so he sold off all his equipment, and then one night a man called to tell him that he had lost the land too, and then he went out to the barn and did it. He hung himself right in there and his family had to move away down south, and they left everything the way it was."

My mouth felt dry as hell. I kept staring at the big red door, waiting for it to swing open. The sun had already begun to set. I looked over my shoulder. There in the distance was the trailer park, not too far away at all. There was a whole line of silver mobile homes cluttered on the horizon, packed tightly together and looking as dull as anything I could ever imagine. I turned back and stared at the red barn. Posted in huge white letters on a black sign were some faded words. I couldn't make them out.

"No trespassers," Lottie whispered. I nodded and cleared my throat, squinting at the silver light that gleamed from inside. "You ready?"

I nodded slowly as Lottie dug her fingers between the two huge red doors and gave them a shove. The whole barn creaked and groaned as more dust erupted from the thin black opening. Lottie stopped pushing and turned to me and winked.

"Do you wanna hold my hand?" she asked with a smile, raising one thin eyebrow.

"No," I mumbled.

"Well, it can be pretty scary," she said with a grin.

"Let's just go in already."

Lottie nodded and gave the doors another push. They howled and finally gave, creaking along their metal tracks, sliding apart.

Dust spun around us like snow as we stepped inside. The place was
dark and damp, with rotting bushels of wet hay, as quiet as a church.

Almost at once, I knew it: *This is His place, the Devil's place,
His place of death.* Above our heads were thousands and thousands
of cobwebs, crossing and crisscrossing in gray translucent cocoons.
There were husks of dead insects left dangling in the light, hung
by their empty shells by long thin strands cast by tiny black spin-
nerettes. I held my breath, gritting my teeth together as I followed
Lottie inside. There was a stack of cut wood, coated in moss now,
piled in one corner. There were some shovels and rakes and scythes
and huge metal tools crowded along the wall. Then there was
something left in the corner, a large brown and black mass at one
side of the barn.

"There it is," Lottie whispered. "The dead horse."

The dead animal was huge. The old horse was a lump of loose
skin that had begun to rot and fester. Flies buzzed everywhere,
darting past our heads, up past the silver cobwebs and back down
to the horse's head. There, along one side of the animal, I could
see some whitish ribs sticking out of its belly. Then I could see its
head, long and thin, resting on its side. It was thrown back with
its huge white teeth open. I felt my stomach go sour. Maybe it was
the heat or maybe all the insects buzzing, but I was sweating now,
sweating right through the bottom of my feet.

"Do you wanna see its guts?"

I shook my head, but this crazy girl just pulled my hand and
led me around the front of the dead animal, pointing at its
innards. The belly was split open, all the organs had spilled
between its legs in a variety of colors and dull, pungent odors.
"There's its intestines," she said, pointing at a white length of flesh
that looked like a bloated worm. "There's its stomach. Look how
big it is." Another yellowed mass, spotted with red and pink and
white dots, hanging out emptily, along its exposed belly. There was

a puddle of dried blood that ran in a ring around its head and belly; some dust and insects rising from its emptied eyes made the damn thing seem still alive.

I was speechless. Lottie gripped my arm and led me deeper inside toward the center of the barn, and then she stopped. She squinted a little at all the dust and then looked up, staring past the silver light into the rafters above.

"That's it. That's where he did it."

I swallowed hard and looked up. There was a thick wooden beam that ran over our heads. It was surrounded by thin eaves of spiderwebs and dust and empty insect bodies. Sunlight split between the boards overhead and poured down across the rafter's edges. There, directly above our heads, was a black mark, thin but still dark, a scrape, a burn caused by the rope rubbing against the beam as Mr. Furnham swung beneath and fought hopelessly for his life. I couldn't move. I stared up, unable to say anything, unable to blink, the dust circling around my head while I imagined the rope cinching around my neck, getting tighter and tighter until I dropped and my neck snapped and my teeth ran against each other in my cheeks and my eyes fell to the back of my head and my hands clenched and my spine became stiff and my stomach hard and I fell straight through my body to my own death. I noticed just then that my hands were trembling and I forced them into my pockets quick.

"Hey, are you okay?" Lottie asked, but I still couldn't move. All I could see was the black mark on the beam overhead. I kept staring up at the rafters, and suddenly, the silver light disappeared and all the shadows vanished. The twilight settled in through the wooden roof, and through all the tiny cobwebs, I thought I could see a face.

There was a face in the dark above us.

A long serpentine body crept along the rafters above us where we stood, with a long black-and-red cloak hanging around its thin arms and legs and head. Its face was like a reptile, a lizard, sharp and thin and mean, with a hood of skin that ran from its skull, darkening its black eyes with shadows it had stolen from midnight. I knew I was seeing it and not seeing it, all at once, recognizing the sound of its steps along the wooden beam, the same quiet inching I had heard every night since we had moved. There, right above my head, was what I was sure was the Devil, dark as blood but quiet as a prayer.

"Are you okay?" Lottie repeated. "Do you wanna leave?" But it was too late. Its long red fingers reached down, brushing against the cold skin of my chest, past my clothes to my poor red heart. Fire began to burn all around my head, flames leapt from my skin and in the air behind me, as the Devil hissed and laughed, the curse, the curse burning bright red in my heart as Lottie pulled me by the arm and through the barn door. I almost started to cry. My teeth were chattering in my head. I stumbled out of the barn and Lottie shook me hard.

"Are you okay?" she shouted.

I nodded, still staring back into the empty red barn.

"Do you wanna go home?"

I nodded again, feeling the whole world darkening and closing around me. Lottie led me by the hand down the dirt path to the wire fence; she helped me over to where she picked up her bike and walked it beside me, peering hard into my eyes like she might start to cry too.

"Do you think you're gonna be sick?" she asked, rolling the bike beside me. "Do you want to stop by my house and rest?"

I do not know why but I nodded, watching the dirt road as it drifted under my feet. I was shaking a little, shivering from all the sweat up and down my back. I leaned against Lottie as she stared in my eyes.

"Here, we're almost there," she said. I followed her down a little road that wound beside another wire fence and led up to her house. Behind me, over my shoulder, was the unlit night. The sky was blue and black and moving slowly with clouds. Behind me was that dark red barn, blossoming with blood, trembling with strange silver lights. I decided not to turn around and look again. Up off the road a little ways was Lottie's house. It was gray and white, a big A-frame farmhouse with a tire-swing hung off a maple tree out front. There were some small white chickens pecking and scurrying about. Their eyes were green in the dark as they squabbled and fluttered beside the front porch.

"Nobody's home," Lottie mumbled, throwing her bike down in the dirt. "We'll go around back." She pulled me by the shirt and led me to the back of the house. There was a gray wood porch and some dark cement stairs that led down to a shadowy basement. Lottie dragged me down the steps and pushed open the rusty basement door. Unafraid, Lottie stepped right into the blackness and found a small silver chain attached to a lightbulb, and gave it a pull. The light snapped awake, swinging from her movement, teetering back and forth on its wire.

"We can sit down here for a while before my dad comes home," she said with a smile, squeezing my arm. As the lightbulb swung, shadows moved all along the walls, creaking back and forth. There were eyes. Thousands of silver eyes. I felt the spit run dry in my mouth. "Trophies," Lottie whispered, still holding my arm. "My dad's a taxidermist. He stuffs them."

There were mounted creatures all around my head. There was a huge purple-and-brown quail mounted as if it was in flight along the wall. There was a black-and-white badger poised at my feet, its huge triangular teeth bared in a snarl. There was a buck's head raised on the wall, its shiny black antlers branching from its brown skull. There were all kinds of fish on brown bits of wood and rock, there was a huge white skull that had been bleached and emptied, there were thick brown and black animal skins that had been stretched along the floor, and there was a huge wooden desk in the corner covered with tools and knives and a hundred glass bottles of all sizes.

"What are those?" I asked.

Inside the round glass jars were silver and green stars, shimmering as the lightbulb swung over our heads.

"Eyes," Lottie whispered.

The lightbulb came to a stop. The shadows went still on the wall.

"Eyes?" I mumbled.

"Glass eyes."

Inside the shiny silver jars were all kinds of glass eyes. Blue eyes, big black eyes, tiny silver eyes, small brown eyes, all smooth and cool as pennies, cold to the touch, but hard and strange and wonderfully mysterious. I held out my palm to feel their weight.

"These are my favorite," Lottie said, opening one of the jars. She dug her fist inside and lifted up a tiny black cloth and pulled out two perfectly round glass eyes. They were big enough for a person, green and hard and reflecting the flickering white light overhead.

"They're beautiful, aren't they?" Lottie smiled, holding the eyes in her tiny white palm. I nodded. Those glass eyes were the most wonderful things I had ever seen. I reached out to touch one. It was cold, cold but warm from Lottie's soft skin. The glass cornea was black and radiant inside, staring out as Lottie moved under the light.

"It's for a person," Lottie whispered. "For Miss Dubuque when she dies."

"Who?"

"The lady who lives on the other side of town. She's going to be stuffed when she dies."

"What?"

"She already paid my daddy to do it. And she wants these green eyes." Lottie placed one in my palm. It fit perfectly in the tiny recess of my hand, rolling around gently as I stared deep inside. They were perfect. They were the perfect death-eyes for a lady who hadn't even died. The thought sent a shiver down my spine.

"What does she want green eyes for?" I asked.

"Who knows? My dad says she's got more money than she knows what to do with."

I held the glass eye in my hand tightly. The thing felt heavy and indestructible against my skin.

"Don't break it now," she whispered. She stared at my face, smiling at my smile. "Nice, huh?"

I nodded again.

"Bet you thought I didn't have anything good at my house," she said. "Here, I better put them back." I held the glass eye for one more moment, then handed it to her, staring as she gently placed it back in the glass jar and covered it with a tiny black blanket, to help the eyes sleep, I guess. In the other corner of the room was a huge brass drum that dripped water into a dirty brown bucket. It dripped, dripped, dripped quietly, splashing against the shiny liquid inside.

"That's my dad's still. Supposed to stay away from that. Moonshine," she said with a wink. I nodded, finally understanding something she had said. One of my mother's worst boyfriends, Joe Brown, who had been a drinker and awful mean to Pill, would take long, angry sips from a gray jug he kept in the trunk of his car. He nearly sent my older brother to the hospital for breaking the radio antenna off his beloved El Dorado. I looked at the still again and suddenly there were heavy, clumsy footsteps pounding against the floor overhead.

"Lottie?!"

I flinched as the footsteps clambered around a little then stopped right above our heads. It sounded like someone dropped a glass, which then shattered on the floor.

"Lottie, get down here and clean up this mess!" the cold, gravelly voice shouted. Lottie froze, then held her breath.

"That's my dad," she said, staring into my eyes. "I'm not supposed to be down here." She sighed, glancing up at the floorboards.

"Lottie?!" he called again. "You better not be down in my things!"

"You better go," she squeaked, opening the back door. I shrugged my shoulders and nodded and ran up the stairs and then around the side of the house, stopping to look over my shoulder to make sure I was alone. There, in the front window, along the faded blue curtains, was a huge shadow, tall and square, the shadow of her father, a man who knew how to use knives to cut and sew and sever. There, behind that window, was a man who kept the eyes of a rich woman in a glass jar on his desk, a man whose voice was hard and mean as if his throat had been overgrown with rust, a man whose own eyes had to be two cold black pits along the side of a long, narrow, serpentine head. Here was a man I had met a dozen time before, men like the kind my mother would bring home once or twice who would then disappear, swearing at her from their cars in the middle of the night. Here was a man I knew how to hate without a single thought. He stood in the front window and watched me run along the dirt as my shadow skittered from dark spot to dark spot, as I hurried down the gravel path and out to the long road that led home.

About half a mile away, I turned around once more and looked back into the darkness, back at Lottie's house, rising there on its little gray hill. Even though I was scared and my legs were weak at the knees, I stopped and turned back and stared hard, kind of hoping that poor girl was following me. For some reason, I felt myself wishing she was right behind me, but she wasn't, she was trapped in that house, like a ghost, hiding there alone in the basement, holding her breath the same way as me.

the birthday surprise

Me, I turned eleven without a sound. It was my first birthday away from Duluth and I felt hopeless spending it with just Pill and my folks. There would be no party with streamers and foil, no stupid party games like *Pin the Tail on the Donkey* or *Spin the Bottle*, no birthday kisses from the older girls on my old block. Worst of all, I guess, there'd be no extra presents, all wrapped up nice and neat in newspaper and bows, no gifts from the other kids in my class who I might have invited. My eleventh birthday was going to be spent with my lousy family in a lousy new town.

It just happened to fall on a Saturday, September 28, so my mother was real sweet and made everyone keep quiet to let me sleep in late. But that damn dog woke me up anyway. I didn't really care. My mom was going to make a huge dinner of all my favorites: pork chops and applesauce and a huge chocolate cake. It all sounded great. I was going to lay around the trailer all day and watch a kung fu movie or an old black-and-white monster show because it was my birthday and French said I could watch what I pleased. But then, about two hours after I woke up, just as I was settling into that lumpy sofa with a nice can of grape soda, well, then there was the most awful surprise, the sound of which started with a knock against the screen door.

"Hello? Is anyone home?!" came the whiny voice. I sat up and rolled my eyes.

"Hello, Marie!" my mother screamed, shoving the chocolate

cake into the oven, dropping her green cooking mitts to the floor. She fumbled at the latch and pushed the screen door open wide. I shook my goddamn head because just then I could smell my aunt's horrible pink perfume like some sort of invisible claw choking my throat. I knew, oh brother, I knew, it was my Aunt Marie and all her stupid kids.

Aunt Marie was my father's older sister. They had both been born and raised in Duluth. By the time my dad was old enough to drive, both of his parents had died, so Aunt Marie thought it was her duty to raise her younger brother, who took more joy in fist fighting and kissing girls than anything else.

At the age of twenty-two, my old man married my mom, according to Pill, because he had knocked her up. Since she was pregnant when she got married and didn't insist on a church wedding, Aunt Marie never forgave my mother. After Pill was born, my old man began doing odd jobs, in addition to working ten to twelve hours a day as an auto mechanic. Mostly, he fenced stolen goods. My mother took care of her baby, cut her neighbors' hair, and started going to church as often as she could. A few years later, I guess they had me, and by then my old man had gotten his trucking license and was working pretty steadily. But the way my aunt saw it, my father had always been a hoodlum and it was only a matter of time before it all caught up with him, leaving us to fend for ourselves, which is exactly what happened.

"Where's the birthday boy?" my aunt asked with a grin. Her face was so big and round that her eyes seemed like two soft black dots pressed into her flesh. Her nose was tiny and snub, and her damn perfume made me sick as she hugged me. I could feel the ridges of her lips as she squeezed me hard and planted the most greasy kiss on my cheek. "How does it feel to be eleven?"

I shrugged my shoulders. There's never an easy answer to get you out of a dumb question like that. Pill grinned like a bastard, shaking his head. He was lucky. He was thirteen, too old and too ugly to be hugged by anyone. But not me. Me, I was still kind of short and pudgy. Aunts and old ladies thought it was real god-damn cute to go and squeeze your cheeks or smother you with their lousy lipsticked mouths. I wiped her makeup off my cheek with my sleeve and stepped aside. Two girls stood behind my aunt, staring at us silently.

"Now don't be bashful. These are your cousins, Dough. This is Hildie. You remember her, don't you?"

Wow. This girl looked like no cousin I ever had. Her hair was short and blond and curled loose down around her ears. She had on a white sweater with a nice plaid skirt and black shoes and thigh-high tights. I guess I hadn't seen Hildie in a few years. Back then, she had been a runny-nosed little goat. Now she was differ-ent. Now this cousin of mine was fourteen. Now she was as pretty and clean as a pearl. Her hands were fidgeting behind her back. *Kissing cousins.* The words popped in my mind. I suddenly couldn't get the thought of kissing Hildie out of my head.

"And this is Pettina," my aunt said. My God. Pettina had got-ten the short end of the ugly stick. Pettina. Apparently, this poor girl had been named after Richard Petty, number 43, the stock car driver. My Uncle Dirk, Aunt Marie's husband, was a real Nascar fan, and according to Pill anyway, he'd had an abscess on his penis and had to have it lanced, and so he only had two daughters, no son, and so my aunt had let her husband pick their youngest's name. Pettina sure was huge. Next to her slender older sister, she looked like some kind of pink pear. She was biting at her nails. Each finger looked like a pork sausage that she kept nibbling at. I began to wonder if, like me, her awful name had led her to all kinds of unhappiness.

"Hello," Pettina kind of snorted all in a huff, like it cost her a lot just to get that single word out. Pettina wore a white-and-pink dress with yellow ribbons in her hair.

"Here you go, sweetheart," my Aunt Marie said, pulling a thin present from her huge black purse. "Just a little something for one of my favorite nephews." This gift looked sad, even wrapped in its dull yellow paper and lousy silver bow. It was too small and thin to be anything good. She handed it to me and I gnashed my teeth.

French pinched his glasses against his nose as he patted me on the back. "Well, go ahead, pal, open it," he whispered. My brother, Pill, shook his head. Not another goddamn wallet. Not another goddamn wallet.

I felt the gift in my hands.

No. There was no luck anywhere in the world.

This gift was going to be another goddamn plastic wallet. I knew it. I could tell. It was too thin, too light to be anything else. I peeled off the yellow paper and forced the worst fake smile on my face. Another goddamn plastic wallet. My lousy Aunt Marie had gotten me a goddamn plastic wallet for every birthday ever since I was about three. I never used them. Heck, I didn't have a thing to put in them. I mean, I was a kid. So they just ended up collecting dust in the bottom drawer of a dresser full of old junk, like shark's teeth and arrowheads and old holy scapulars I had forgotten how to roll. This year's wallet was vinyl brown, not even simulated leather, with gold trim. There, embossed in one corner, was the single word, *Hawaii*. I didn't even bother to sigh.

Of course, Pill let out a squeal. He laughed and grinned. Sure, this was all a regular riot.

"We got that for you when we went to the islands last summer," my aunt said, smiling. I nodded, not saying a damn word. "We know how old you're getting and a man needs a good wallet." Or one hundred crappy plastic ones, I thought.

"Say thanks, Dough," French whispered.

I shook my head like I suddenly forgot how to hear.

"Say thanks," he whispered again. I clamped my teeth together and folded my lips in. There was a dull silence in the air, waiting, waiting, waiting for me to say *thank you* or *thanks* or *what a great gift, gee, thanks*, but I didn't say a damn word, I just held my breath until my dumb dog, Shilo, marched right up and licked the back of my hand.

"What in the world is that creature?" my aunt whispered.

"That's our dog," I grunted, scratching the top of its ugly head. Shilo rubbed its face against my leg and then sniffed at Aunt Marie's feet. Its empty eye rubbed against her fat gray thigh as it laid its big paw on her chest.

"It certainly is the ugliest animal I've ever seen." Aunt Marie frowned, shaking her head. "What happened to it?"

"It got hit by a truck."

"June, what kind of dog is that?" my aunt called to my mother in the kitchen.

"Oh, you know, the boys found it so we gave it a home," she called back.

"Certainly doesn't seem healthy to have a dog like that just roaming around."

My older brother shook his head and got up off the sofa. He pulled on his gray hooded sweatshirt, looking like he was about to leave.

"Where do you think you're going?" I asked in a kind of plea.

"Someone needs to take the dog for a walk," he lied, pulling on Shilo's big black collar. That bastard Pill had never taken the dog for a walk before. But now, since my aunt was there, he was looking for any way out he could find.

"Why don't all you kids take the dog for walk? It'll give us adults some time to talk," my mother said, stirring some punch in a big plastic bowl.

"That sounds nice. It will give the adults a chance to catch up," my aunt said, grinning falsely.

"Christ," Pill muttered with a frown.

"Pill, watch your mouth!" my mother hollered. My brother shook his head and kicked the screen door open and all four of us stepped outside. The sky was blue and bright with big clouds that hung over our heads like ice cream. Shilo hopped down the stairs and back around the trailer to the wide field that began just a few hundred feet away. There, right in the distance, was the haunted barn, a dark red dot sticking out from the blue sky like a scar. I knew that in the barn lived the Devil, who was the cause of the worst nightmares I had ever had in my life. I turned from its awful sight and stared down at Hildie's black shoes.

"I'll wait here," Pettina said with a frown, taking a seat on our gray cement steps.

"Fine by me, stay here if you want," Pill muttered, pulling his blue stocking cap down over his scab. He dug into his pockets and pulled out a pack of smokes. He kept mumbling to himself, kicking at the dirt as he fumbled for a match. I paid my brother no mind. I kept staring at my cousin Hildie's black shoes. Her socks ended just below her bare knees. That white space, between the bottom of her skirt and the top of her knees, seemed pretty perfect to me.

"Did you ever smoke?" Pill asked Hildie, lighting up a cigarette. He took a long drag and let the smoke trickle out of his mouth, like he was some sort of real tough guy.

"Duh," Hildie said with a smile, plucking the cigarette from his lips. She fit it into her tiny mouth and smiled, taking a short drag and exhaling like a pro, without choking on a lung or coughing up any smoke, the way I guess I usually did. "Did you ever smoke grass?" she asked, taking another drag. I felt my eyebrows shoot up over my forehead. Lord. Grass? One of my mother's boyfriends, Lenny, used to come over and smoke it all the time. Me and my brother would sit at the top of the stairs and try to get high that way but it never did any good. "Did you ever?" she asked again. I guess I was surprised. Maybe my cousin wasn't such a clean little pearl at all. Her lips were curled tight around the cigarette, making her whole round face seem kind of shiny and a little older. Maybe she was just like the other high school girls I'd see walking home in town; smoking with their thin hands bent just at the wrist, laughing their fake laughs, talking about who did it with who. It made me want to kiss her even worse. "You've never smoked grass?"

"Sure," Pill lied. "I've done it a couple of times."

Hildie finished off the smoke and flicked it into the dirt. Then she just took a seat, right in the grass, and spread her skirt over her thighs. She ran her hand over her sweater and undid the top snap. Then she reached down inside the sweater and pulled out a pink stick of bubble gum from beside the palest skin I had ever seen. She folded the gum inside her mouth and smiled. My God, this girl was trying to be cute as hell. My older brother stared at her hard, not saying a word. His hands were dug into his coat pockets. He looked kind of worried and kind of confused.

"I'm going back to the house," he said with a frown. Hildie shrugged her shoulders in reply.

My brother backed away slow like he was trying to think of something else to say, but then ran out of space to walk. He just shook his head and turned away.

"What do you guys do around do here for fun?" Hildie asked, snapping the gum in her mouth.

"We don't do anything," I said weakly. Her nose twitched a little when she blew a perfect pink bubble. Her lips made a gentle smacking sound as the bubble snapped and then disappeared back in her mouth.

"Do you got a girlfriend or anything?"

"Nope," I said with a frown. More than anything in my life, I wanted to take her hand and sit down right there and touch her hair.

"Did you ever French kiss anybody?"

"Nnn . . . no." I had wanted to lie at first, but then it felt like she had pulled the words right out of my mouth. My lips felt dry as I finally got up enough nerve and sat down beside her.

"Why is that?" she asked.

"I don't know."

"Do you ever practice?"

"No."

"No? Never?"

"No."

Of course, I had seen a million naked girls in a million different nudie magazines and imagined kissing them all over, but not one of them had been real.

"I practice all the time," she said. "All you have to do is kiss the back of your hand." She held hers up and smiled, then closed her eyes and began kissing it very, very slowly. I shrugged my shoulders and lifted my hand and started doing the same thing. It felt awful corny to me.

"No, here, you're supposed to open your mouth a little." She took the back of my hand and so gently, so softly pressed her lips there. I suddenly felt like I was going to explode and so I hurried away, tripping over my clumsy feet.

"Okay, well, thanks," I said, unsure of what else to say.

"You all ready for dinner?" my cousin Pettina called from around the side of our trailer. I nodded nervously and walked around to the front door. Pill sat there on the steps with a scowl, tightening his fingers into tiny white fists at his side. Shilo sat before him, its head in his lap. I could hear an argument of some

kind inside the trailer, somebody was shouting, but quietly, as my
older brother put his hand against my shoulder to keep me from
going in.

"I don't know why they don't just run off! Young boys like
that! Lucky they don't end up to be criminals!" came my aunt's
awful voice.

But my mother and French didn't say a word.

"I don't suppose you've been taking them to church?"

"Sunday school every week, Marie," my mother answered,
which was the truth. Every Sunday morning Pill and I spent an
hour with Mrs. Heget, the deacon's wife, and a roomful of other
heathens who didn't know the difference between wrong and
right.

"Well, I'd like to know what goes on here—really, I would.
Have you two even *thought* about getting married?" my Aunt
Marie hissed.

"We're not getting married, Marie," my mother said, banging
a pot or pan. "French here is the best man, the best man I've ever
met, but we both agreed—"

"Well, it's not right, the two of you living like this, with those
boys around. They're very impressionable."

By then Pill's face had turned bright red. He hated Aunt
Marie worse than me, I think.

"The whole thing's not right," Marie argued. "It just isn't
respectable."

Pill gritted his teeth, clenching his fingers tight to the bone.
He stood up and spat hard onto our neighbor Mrs. Garnier's back
porch. I pressed my face up against the screen for a peek. My aunt
had her fat arms crossed, hovering beside my mother, who was finishing the chocolate cake.

"And what about their father? What do you think he'd feel
about all of this?" Aunt Marie mumbled through her perfect white

teeth. I turned away from the screen and shook my head. My older brother threw open the door. He ran into the trailer and snarled, staring up into my aunt's fat white face.

"Get out!" my brother shouted. "Get out now."

"Pill!" my mother gasped.

"I mean it. If French is being too quiet to do it, then I will."

"Pill!" French hollered, shaking his head.

"Get out! You don't talk to my mom like that. My dad would have never stood for that."

"Pill," my mother muttered. "Not another word."

"Well, I see exactly how it is!" my Aunt Marie shot back. Her face was all flustered and bright red. She held her hand over her chest like she had never heard such harsh words before. "It's no wonder these boys cause all the trouble they do. In a madhouse like this, I'm surprised they're not worse off!" My fat aunt fumbled around for her purse, then stood by the screen door. "This unclean life is not worth living!" she shouted. "And you're all unclean as rags! Filthy rags!" She turned and wobbled down our front steps and back into her brown station wagon. Her daughters followed her, not saying a word. Of course, Pettina had begun to cry, but my other cousin, Hildie, just frowned and turned, popping a pink bubble in her mouth, rolling her eyes as my aunt pulled their car back down the gravel drive and onto the road. I guess there was something so pretty and kind of resigned in my cousin Hildie's face. The station wagon turned in the wrong direction, started down the road, then stopped, backed up, and started in the right direction, passing us again. Pill and I stood on the front porch and waved.

My mother was sobbing now, her face all red and full of tears. She locked herself in the bathroom, crying, running the water so we couldn't hear how bad she was feeling. French shook his head, staring out the open screen door, then down at his open can of beer.

"Jesus, Pill, what did ya do that for?" he asked.

Pill stood beside me, still clenching his fists at his side. "You weren't gonna say anything."

"There's a time and a place, pal. A time and a place, and this sure as hell wasn't the time."

My older brother glared at French hard and then turned and disappeared into our room. I fell onto the sofa, staring at the blank TV screen.

"Sorry about all this, Dough." French frowned. "It ain't right to ruin a man's birthday. This didn't have anything to do with you at all."

Me, I just shrugged my shoulders and glared at the blank screen. That's exactly how I felt. I guess I just didn't even care.

"I'm gonna go talk to your mom," he muttered, patting me on my head. My dumb dog came and sat beside me and laid its ugly face on my lap. I scratched its fur, rubbing my finger along the empty space where its one black eye should have been. Suddenly I felt sure of something. In that moment, right there, I felt like maybe my aunt had been right. Maybe my brother and me were doomed. Maybe one of the reasons I didn't have any friends was because of how bad we both acted. I stared down at my dog, who, like always, had fallen asleep in my lap. Its hind legs were kicking in a dream, maybe some nightmare of being chased by something. Its good eye flickered around under its white eyelid, as it breathed heavily against my legs. I guess I shut my eyes for a minute and felt like crying, crying alone on the lousy couch because my birthday had been awful and because I didn't have a single friend in the entire world. It would have been a fine way to end the worst birthday I had ever had, but I didn't start crying; I just closed my eyes and tightened my hands into hard white fists to keep it all in.

A knock at the door startled me right out of my gloom.

"Hello, Dough," Lottie whispered, pressing her big white forehead against the screen. "Are you home?"

That girl sure was crazy.

I smiled and nodded my head and stepped out onto the porch. It looked like she had ridden to my trailer as fast as she could. Her face was all sweaty and her pigtails were coming loose on the side of her head. She was leaning against the porch railing with something in her hands, something hidden, closed tightly between her tiny fingers. Her pink bike sat at the bottom of our gray steps. She was smiling, smiling big and wide, winking at me.

"I came because I have something for you," she whispered, leaning in close to me. "I didn't wrap it up in paper or anything, but I hope you still like it."

And then she opened her tiny hands just below my face. There, in the rounded part of her pink palm was the most mysterious thing I had ever seen. A green glass eye. The glass eye that belonged to the richest lady in town. I felt my mouth drop open and my throat drying up. I didn't know what to say.

"But . . ."

"I don't think my dad will notice it's gone. That lady isn't gonna die for at least another forty years."

She placed the eye in my hand, her fingers moving against my skin. There, cool and strange as a dream, I could feel its weight and gravity resting in my palm.

"I shouldn't take this. If your dad found out—"

"Shush," Lottie cut me off with a smile. "It's yours now."

I wanted to say something really nice, to let her know how it was the best birthday gift I had ever gotten, but the words wouldn't come out. I felt lucky enough to muster, "This thing is neat as hell."

Lottie just smiled, all red-faced and embarrassed, I guess. She didn't say another word, just hopped down my front porch steps to her awful pink bike and rode on home, nodding her head and singing to herself.

I could not believe that green glass eye was all mine.

I held it in my two hands. I laid on the sofa and placed it in my palms and watched it roll on my skin, glittering with light, shining with some sort of indescribable beauty. I didn't know why I thought it was so lovely but I did. I hid it in my front pants pocket as my mother and French came out of the bathroom. My mother's face was still a little red. French had his hand on her shoulder. After a little while, he called us to dinner and tried to serve us as best as he could, tying my mother's blue-and-white apron around his waist and spooning out helpings of her badly burned food. My brother stayed holed up in our room, missing the cake, which sagged all on one side and wasn't really cooked. But I ate it all, I didn't give a damn; I forced it all in my mouth with a smile, thinking of the glass eye and Lottie, too, maybe.

After dinner I sat out on the porch by myself, grinning at the way the eye seemed to glimmer and glow, wondering if there was some way to use it to tell the future or to read minds. After a while, I kissed my mother and French shook my hand and I went off to bed, careful not wake my older brother, who laid curled up in his bunk, facing the wall. I slipped under the covers and placed that glass eye right on the sheets above my chest, staring at it as the light from my bedroom windows made it glow with perfect sight. It really was the best gift anyone could have ever given me. I guess there was something so special there, something powerful and mysterious. Sure, there was nothing I could really do with it. And that poor girl was probably going to get the whipping of her life for stealing it. But there was something about it, something otherworldly in that green and white and blown glass, something in its shape, something I could see and stare at, imagining a future of different moments and a world of faraway possibilities. I decided

I would show my older brother and hopped out of bed, holding it beside his head.

"Look at what I got," I whispered.

"What is it?"

"A glass eye."

"That's stupid," Pill mumbled, rolling back over. He coughed a little, then yanked the covers up over his head. My dumb dog sniffed the eye once, then slid its face beneath the covers, crowding me.

I didn't really care. I placed the glass eye on the sill of the window beside my bed and stared at it until I fell asleep, sure of all the ways everything would be different for me.

When morning came and the eye was still there, gleaming, I stared at it, and for the first time in a long while I felt lucky, lucky for having something no else in the world had. I decided it would be my good luck charm, and that I would carry it around with me all the time. I decided it would be our secret, mine and Lottie's.

I let her hold it whenever she wanted to, and she did, keeping it in her lap every day during lunch. When she'd hand it back to me, warm from her touch, I would put it back in my pocket, glad to finally have a secret with somebody.

the dollar-eighty-nine story

"Push not pull, pale-face."

I pulled on the big silver door handle for the hundredth time, my hands trembling in nervous confusion. The old Injun grumbled at me from behind the counter, shaking his head from beyond the glass door.

"Push! Push, fool! Push!"

I kind of shrugged my shoulders and gave the door a good solid push, smiling at the tall, red-faced Injun as he shook his head and turned away. The bell above the door rattled when I stepped inside, right past the sign that read, *Real-Life Indian Artifacts,* standing before the stacks of old Mars Bars and stale candy that lined the shelf in front of the gas station's counter. Behind me there was a dusty aisle of mud flaps with the outlines of silver girls glued to them, a shelf of miniature Minnesota spoons and shot glasses, and a whole row of realistic-looking porcelain statues of cougars with their young and wolves howling at the moon. Chief's Filling Station was the only goddamn place in town that would sell cigarettes or dirty magazines to minors. It was about three miles away from our trailer park and a good hike even on a clear day, but depending purely on the mood of the Chief, the owner and only clerk who was almost always drunk, you might walk all that way and not return with a pack of Marlboros or a glossy issue of *High Society*. He was the only Injun I ever actually knew, except the ones from TV, and those were about as real as the naked ladies spread out in the nudie magazines my brother and me tried to steal. Today would be my first time trying to buy smokes without Pill. I had been eleven for nearly two full weeks, almost a teenager, almost a young man. I guess I thought the chances of me getting the smokes were about as likely as me becoming an astronaut, but I felt like I owed it to myself to give it a try.

"Gimme a pack of Marlboros," I kind of stammered, staring up into the Chief's thin, porous face, which was wrinkled like an old tree. There was his big bulbous knob right between a pair of eyes that jutted out of his hard skin. There were all kinds of crazy lines running down and around his face like thick branches. His pupils were bloodshot and red as hell. He stank like an open bottle of sour mash. He had long black hair all knotted behind his head in a ponytail, gray along the edges, that ran down his back. He wore a black shirt with a string of beads looped around his neck. He would have been spooky as hell if he wasn't drunk, and I sure wouldn't have tried buying smokes from him if I ever thought he might actually be standing behind that counter sober.

"Show me some proof of age," the Chief grunted, all in slow, single-syllable words. I didn't know what to do. I thought that kids like me were the only ones keeping him in business.

"Oh, c'mon, man, don't be a drag."

His gnarled-up face remained cold and expressionless. He pulled a silver flask from his back hip pocket, uncapped it, and took a long drink. A single bead of liquor ran down between two hard wrinkles on his chin and disappeared. "Do not think I do not know how old you really are," he whispered, leaning over the counter. "You are nothing but a baby to me." He let out a loud thick laugh that echoed in his wide throat.

"Oh, c'mon, Chief, stop busting my balls. I'm old enough already."

"No. No, you have no idea about being old. What do you know? Hmm? What do you know?"

I rubbed my face with frustration.

"Listen, man, I just want some smokes."

"You listen, little boy, and I will tell you a story about what it means to be old—old enough to call yourself a man."

He took another shot from his flask and leaned his red face close to mine. I could feel his hot breath on the bridge of my nose.

"Three days before my thirteenth birthday, my father took me out of our home and into the woods. My father was a great warrior and chief of our people, he was on the State Council for Indian Rights. He had helped get a new school built on our reservation and hot water into our homes. His white name was John Cloud. My people called him Great Gray Cloud."

The Chief's eyes looked black and stern. The folds on his face tightened into a serious plain of red flesh as he went on with this unrelenting bullshit. Don't get me wrong, as far as the adults in town went, the Chief seemed like one of the few of them I wouldn't want to set fire to. I guess he had a kind of nobility about him.

"My father took me out into the woods to observe an old ritual among our people. The passing of a boy into manhood."

He took a swig from the flask. I didn't look away. I wanted to see if he would cough. He did.

"He lit a sacrificial fire and asked the great earth spirits to welcome me into manhood, to help me break from my childish ways and become a leader of our people the way his father had. My father took me to the sweat lodge and we sat there for two days and prayed to Coyote and the Four Winds, and there we had visions and he told me of the promise I would fulfill to our people. On my birthday, my father took me on a great hunt."

His eyes were twinkling like stars in the sky, far away and silver and blue. He was drunk now for sure.

"There was an old wolf that had been raiding our chicken coop ever since I was a child. This was no ordinary wolf. No. This was a great spirit wolf with the marking of Coyote, the trickster. He would leave only two paw prints, side by side in the snow where he tracked. Two prints like a man. He would wring the chickens' necks but not touch their eggs, and when my mother would collect the eggs and crack them open, there would only be blood. My father had been tracking the wolf for years. He was a great hunter. He would set traps for the wolf, and when he would go to check them, they would always be empty. He had raised a whole litter of dogs to track the wolf. The pack he had raised fought with the wolf a dozen times, but the wolf would always escape. Only once had my father ever really seen the wolf, and it was that time I was ten and he had taken me with him to hunt pheasant. This all made it very clear for him. My father said that the wolf was waiting. The wolf was waiting for me to be old enough to hunt it."

I guess I was starting to get pretty interested as the Chief took another swig.

"On my thirteenth birthday, my father and I set out to hunt the wolf. He brought his dogs along and I had my mighty Winchester .22 and he had his compound bow and we tracked the two-footed wolf down into a shallow valley all covered with snow. Two paw prints ran down the valley, side by side. The walls of the valley were too steep for the wolf to climb out of. The valley ended in an old brick dam that was also too steep to climb. My heart was filled with fire. I felt humbled. If I shot and killed the wolf, I would be made a man. If I somehow missed, I would forever lose my father's respect. My father stopped at the ridge of the valley and nodded to me. He unleashed the pack of dogs and they ran down the ridge. They tore through the snow. They barked loudly. They disappeared into the darkness. They had the great wolf trapped. I could hear it. I marched down the trail and then looked back at my father. He stood there like a mountain, with his hands in his pockets. He could tell me nothing else. I was on my own. I switched off the safety on my gun. The mighty barrel had turned to sweat in my cold hands. The dogs were silent now. The cold white wind was silent now. All was quiet. Everything was waiting. Would I be made a man like my father? Or would I fail and bring shame upon myself?"

I guess my own hands were covered in sweat too. I couldn't move. The Chief leaned in even closer, his big gnarled nose nearly touching my ear.

"The dark shadows of the valley fell upon my back. There was the end of the valley. There was the old dam. There were my father's dogs, who were silent. They sat there completely still. They sat beside one another in a kind of half-moon. The wolf was there, in the darkest part of the valley. He was white and silver. He was black. His head was huge. His front haunches may have came up to my shoulders. His snout was long and sharp. His eyes were the deepest blue. He stood completely still, staring right back into my eyes, his sides breathing with the cold in my chest.

"Then he moved. A silent move, a move of grace. He ran through the dogs, right up the middle of the valley toward me. I felt my finger along the trigger. I felt his heart in my throat. His eyes were my own eyes. His breath was my own breath. The wolf bounded right before me. I closed my eyes. I heard him speak. I pulled the trigger. There was no sound. There was nothing. Then there was only a sigh, like snow falling on soft ground. The sky above me turned black. The wind whipped against my face. The game had ended and I turned back."

My face was bright red as I waited for him to finish. But he was silent. I tapped on the counter, staring up at him.

"What the hell happened? Did ya kill it?" But the Chief only leaned back, lowering his head. His eyes sparkled a little, then turned black. It was like something had welled up in his face that made him look fine and dull and old. He stared down at me and shook his head, then pulled a pack of Marlboros from behind the counter and slid them across to me.

"Dollar eighty-nine," he mumbled.

"What? Well, what the hell happened? Did ya kill it?"

"Do you want the cigarettes or not?"

I guess I stood there, dumbfounded, looking up into his dark face. He didn't even see me anymore. I placed my money on the counter, still stunned. He hit the cash register and placed the money inside. I backed toward the door, feeling all the weight of my body in the back of my knees. The little bell above the door rang as I pulled it open.

"I killed the wolf," I heard him whisper to himself. He let out a hard little cough that made my lungs hurt in my chest. "That was the worst day of my life."

The cigarettes felt like a thousand pounds in my hand. They were slick with sweat. Somehow I was already outside my trailer. Somehow I had walked home already.

There was nowhere else in town I would even consider trying to buy cigarettes or dirty magazines from after that. Even if some other place would have sold them to me, the Chief's Filling Station had some kind of hold on my heart. I used to go there about every other day after school, buy some smokes like an old pro or maybe just a candy bar, and old Chief would always be there behind the counter, a little drunk but as stern-faced as a priest. He was one of the few people in that lousy town who seemed like he had any kind of heart at all, drunk as he may have been.

"Do you know what is out there waiting for me?" the Chief

whispered one day. I had placed a Mars Bar on the counter.

I stared up into his gray face and shook my head.

"Nothing. No one," he grunted. He took a long pull from his flask, licking his lips as he swallowed. "No peace. No sleep. No father, no mother, no wife. No baby. There is no great meeting place. There are no feasts. Those are poor dreams a fool believes so that he may feel better about being deceased."

I shrugged my shoulders. "You don't believe in heaven?" I asked him.

"No." He hit the *Sale* button and the cash register drawer flew open. "If there was a heaven, it would be a cold, cold place. There is nothing good waiting for anyone when they die. There is only your fear. Only your fear, which is cold and black."

I counted out my change, dime, dime, quarter, and slid it across the counter. His breath seemed to gather around him in great gray fumes. He was drunk worse than I had ever seen him before. Then I noticed something. There was a tiny blue baby shoe sitting on the counter beside the register. There were two small silver bells tied to the ends of the laces. Those laces were untied and frayed, dangling and worn. The rest of the shoe looked nearly new. I stared at it, biting my lip. The Chief looked me in the face, then pushed the shoe away, dropping it in a drawer.

"My boy," he whispered. His eyes were filling with tears. He began to scare the hell out of me. He reached across the counter and grabbed my shoulder. "How old are you?" he said between breaths.

"Eighteen," I muttered. His eyes were dark black and huge. His lips were pink and looked dry enough to bleed.

"How old are you?" the Chief shouted now, shaking me hard.

"Eleven!" I let out like a coward, dropping the candy bar from my hand.

"Eleven," he said with a smile. "You've had eleven years to

yourself. Eleven years to breathe." He held me in place and I felt my knees knocking together. His face seemed enormous and very wrinkled. His skin branched out all over his face in thick grooves of flesh.

"There is nothing to believe," he whispered. Thick tears broke down his cheeks. "Tell me what am I supposed to believe . . ."

His fingers were digging into my shoulder, gripping my collar. My bottom lip was trembling. My eyes were filling with tears too. I guess it felt like he was right inside my heart, like what he was saying was coming right from my dreams.

"There is no good. No good in this place, is there? There are things you love and things you have that all go and burn and die. There are things that are part of you and your heart that fall to pieces and leave you stranded like a dog."

He shook me once.

"Tell me what will help me . . ." he muttered.

"Please just let me go," I whimpered.

"Tell me what will help me . . ."

"You're hurting me," I whispered, trying to pull free. He let go, his long, thin fingers turning loose as I tripped backwards, falling to the floor.

"I am sorry," he said quietly. "I am sorry. Take whatever you want. Take it all. You can have anything you want."

He laid his head down on the counter and began to sob. I slowly pulled myself to my feet. His voice was like an old woman's as his shoulders shook. His sobs were dry and hard and empty. I began to back toward the door. My fingers moved along the silver door bar. I began to pull it open slowly. The bell above it gave a little twinkle.

The Chief lifted his head and stared into my eyes. "Don't go to sleep. There are so many ghosts waiting for you there."

I felt a cold shiver run down my spine as I ran out and then back to the trailer park and into my bedroom, trembling under my covers until my older brother, Pill, came home and told me to get lost so he could look at his dirty magazines alone. I went outside and crawled under the trailer, right between the thick gray cement blocks, smoking a cigarette, waiting for all the mobile homes around me to light up and for my mother to call, *Supper's ready*, and for my brother to give me a shot to the arm so that none of that whole afternoon would have felt the way it did and everything would seem okay again, but it didn't happen. My mother called, then again, and I just sat under the trailer until French came out and asked me, "Are you okay, pal?" and I nodded and felt all the ghosts in the world moving toward me in the dark that had just fallen.

"Do you believe in ghosts?" I asked my older brother as we washed up for dinner.

"What, are you some kind of baby?" he snickered, rubbing his wet hands on his T-shirt.

"No, I just . . ." I didn't finish and Pill stared me in the face and squinted a little.

"There's no such thing as spooks," he said.

"What about Jesus and all that? Souls and all that?"

"Jesus. You mean spirits? You mean like . . . Dad?" he asked.

I nodded.

"He's dead. There's nothing else to it." He wiped his hands on his shirt once more.

"But you think he's in heaven, right?"

"I dunno." Pill's face looked mean. "He died stealing something. I dunno how it all works. He could be in heaven. He might be in hell too. It doesn't matter. It ain't your problem." He patted me on the shoulder and then frowned.

"But you said there ain't ghosts, right? So what about God? You believe in Him still, right?"

"I don't know. I don't think He does anyone any good but Himself." Pill opened the bathroom door and stepped out.

My hands were still wet. I sat on the toilet wiping my hands on the towel. My older brother didn't understand. I was convinced that we were both cursed because of our dad, because of what he had done, and how he had died. I was pretty sure that the Chief was right. I was pretty sure that there were ghosts all around and that sooner or later they'd catch up with me.

"Dough, you coming to dinner?" my mother called.

"Yeah!" I shouted back. I hung up the towel and made completely sure I was out of the bathroom before I reached around blindly and flicked off the light.

the king of the tango

Out of nowhere, I began to wake up every night and hear the same strange song, usually just after I had fallen asleep. I'd push open the red curtains that hung from the window in our bedroom and stare out at the new silver trailer next to ours, watching as a square shadow moved in the dark to the *beat-beat-beat* of the night. Usually at about midnight, the old man next door would put on an old tango record and shut off all the lights and then begin dancing, sometimes naked, sometimes not, swaying alone in the quiet dark. His name was El Rey del Perdito. In the day, I'd seen his long gray face and full black pompadour, hair that didn't look like it belonged on his withered old head. He was large with big shoulders like an old athlete and moved very slow, except when he was dancing, and then he was like dynamite. I guess I had never seen anything like it before in my life. We had lived in that trailer park for nearly two months, and by then I had just about refused to be amazed by anything.

From my bedroom window, I could hear his bare feet as they shuffled and slid across his tile floor. The mobile home would rock a little as he moved, stepping in time to the exotic music that boomed from behind his shiny yellow curtains. I would see the flicker of candles along the windows and his shadow moving on the walls, back and forth, back and forth, swaying in time to the rhythm of the music and his very sad heart, his wide feet sliding across the floor as his thin shadow spun about.

One night I heard French get up and mutter to my mother, "Jesus. It's past midnight. The damn boys have school tomorrow. Doesn't he have any goddamn consideration?"

I kept listening, hearing El Rey's feet move as the tango singer's voice peaked, shaking the windows in the old man's mobile home. I flinched as I caught a glimpse of his bare back when he crossed in front of his window. Pill snored in the bunk bed above mine, and I guess I was afraid to wake him, to let him know what was happening.

"That's it. I'm going over there!" French yelled.

"Oh, don't be silly," my mother said. "It's fine."

"It's fine?"

"It's nice. It's kind of romantic."

I rolled my goddamn eyes and laid back down in my bed. I was pretty sure I heard my mother let out a laugh. I shook my head and pulled the pillow over my face as they started doing it, the thin walls of our trailer rocking with their movements. I gritted my teeth and stuck the corners of my pillow in my ears. Heck, I wasn't stupid. I knew my mother and French did it. But having to listen to it, right in the middle of the goddamn night, and with the old man next door dancing and singing along with the record, it was too much. I shouted some curse word and then French laughed, my mother trying to stifle her giggle.

I woke up the next morning, got dressed, ate some cereal, and watched as my mother gave French a long kiss goodbye right in front of us. She sighed as he took his lunch bag out of the fridge and disappeared, hurrying out the screen door to work. Pill-Bug sat beside me, gulping some cereal down, dripping milk all over his shirt.

"What the hell was that last night?" I mumbled.

"What?" My mother glared at me with a funny look in her eyes.

"What was all that noise?" I was trying to embarrass her so that they'd never think about doing it while I was around ever again.

"The new neighbor next door," my mother said, "is a dancer."

"No, not that," I grunted, staring my mother cold in the eyes. "The other noise."

"What other noise?" My mother dropped her gaze and poured herself some coffee. She looked over her nails as if they were the most interesting things in the world.

"You know, the other noise."

"I'm sure I don't know what you mean." She took a sip of coffee very smugly, still staring at her nails.

"C'mon, Mom, you know what I mean. It's disgusting."

"Excuse me?"

"You're grossing me out," I mumbled.

"Well," her face became bright red, her eyes still fixed on the rim of her coffee cup, "I am sorry. I forgot whose house this is."

"Yeah. It's gross as hell," Pill grunted, staring her in the face. "You're supposed to be an adult and all that. Can't you wait until we aren't around to do that stuff? It's sickening. Really."

"Well, some of the things you boys do gross me out a little, to be quite honest. All those magazines in your bedroom. Don't you think that makes me feel a little grossed out?"

Pill's face went bright red. My mother looked right at him and he lowered his head, finishing off his breakfast in one quick gulp.

"Those are Pill's," I said.

"I'm gonna be late for school," my brother said and threw his cereal bowl into the sink. He grabbed his books and shot out of the trailer. My mother smiled a little, whistling to herself, washing my brother's dirty bowl. She scrubbed it clean, then placed it in the dish rack to dry. Her eyes met mine silently. There was nothing else to say. I looked away, shoving another spoonful of

Crunchy-O's in my mouth. The lines of her shoulders were soft and round as she wrung the dish towel and stared out the kitchen window, still whistling to herself.

Then she turned, kind of studying me, and said, "After school, you better come by the parlor." She stood beside me, touching my unruly brown hair. "You really need a trim. Okay?"

"Okay," I said, hoping she'd forget. But when I ran out after Pill a few minutes later, she mentioned it again, and I knew better than to ignore her, unless she started revealing all the terrible secrets she had on me.

I did not like the beauty parlor. All the women there made me want to squirm. With the cackle of those ladies' awful cigarette-tinged voices, and their gossip, and their whispering, it was enough to make me squeal in pure agony. The Curl Up 'N Dye Beauty Parlor was located in town a few blocks from the Pig Pen supermarket and a few streets over from the hardware store. One Thursday every month, my mother would cut my damn hair and I'd have to endure that awful pink parlor filled with cheap spray perfume from blue tear-shaped bottles and fork-toothed gossip I wasn't supposed to understand.

"Be still, darlin'," my mother warned, snipping the scissors along, tickling my neck.

Clip.

A lock of brown hair curtsied to the tile floor.

"Well, when I told Danny, my first husband, God rest his soul, that I was pregnant, he said, 'What if I don't want a kid?'" Mrs. Larue whispered this from under her green cat's-eyes glasses, her mouth full of smoke. To me, it seemed like Mrs. Larue had had at least ten million ex-husbands. Heck, I wasn't even sure if they were all dead or if she had just been divorced half-a-million times, but from all the different stories she had about different men, I kind of guessed her marriages only lasted a week or so. Mrs. Larue sat in a silver salon chair, smoking, her legs up on another vacant seat. Her face was narrow and white and her own hair was like a great blue tuft of cotton candy stuck in place by a thick coat of hairspray. Mrs. Larue wasn't so much beautiful as she was glamorous. There were big black-and-white photos of her pasted up all around the store from when she was younger and had been a winner of the Miss Teen Minnesota beauty pageant. Her hair looked exactly the same, like she had applied a thick coat of makeup and some styling spray to her face and hair to preserve it for all eternity. Mrs. Larue also wore the tightest pants I ever saw, bright pants too, like polka-dot pink or bright green that showed her wide, divine hips.

"So I say, 'Danny, if you don't want a kid, you better split town now because it is on its way, honey, and there ain't a damn thing to do about it now.'"

"Men."

"You can't change 'em and you can't shoot 'em."

"Oh, you can shoot them."

All the ladies nodded and laughed and then took drags on their smokes at exactly the same time. There was Mrs. Larue in the silver salon chair, and Mrs. Darve in the chair beside her, and the deacon's fat wife, Mrs. Heget, who didn't even work there but stopped by afternoons just to gossip. She was standing next to my mother, admiring the job she was doing.

"My husband, Lucky, he was the most stubborn man you ever met," my mom said. I sat up, listening, turning a little in the metal chair. "He's the one who insisted on their names," she whispered.

Mrs. Larue nodded knowingly. "Oh, I can believe it."

"We had an awful row about it. *Pill-Bug*. What type of name is that for a boy?"

"It's not a family name?" Mrs. Heget asked. Her fat face was crossed over a frown.

"That's what we argued about. I asked him if it was some relative or friend or someone he was naming our boy after, but he said, 'No, I just like the way it sounds.' I said, 'Why do you want to name your first born that?' And he said, 'A name like that will make the boy tough.' I guess he named Dough here for the same reason."

"What?" Mrs. Heget said. "I don't think I understand."

"He figured these boys would grow up tough and mean from other kids teasing them about their names all the time. He thought they'd get in plenty of fights and then they'd have to grow up strong and learn exactly how to be men or die trying. He was a fool. My Lucky, oh my, he was a fool all right. He's been dead for four years now."

"Men," Mrs. Larue mumbled.

"Do you know what?" Mrs. Darve whispered. She was thin and had a pale white face. She didn't have eyebrows. Instead, she'd draw them on for herself. Two deep brown smudge marks than ran over her blue eyes. It didn't make a damn bit of sense to me. Mrs. Darve smiled. Her fingers pulled the cigarette away from her mouth. "Last weekend when I went over to Aubrey to visit my sister for a day, I forgot to make a dinner for Eddie and so he ate half a jar of mayonnaise instead."

All the ladies let out horrible, wheezy laughs all at once.

Mrs. Larue grinned. "Men," she said again.

I gripped the silver swiveling chair tightly, squirming under the white plastic apron that fit me like a dress, tied too tight around my neck and too long for the rest of my body. My mother snipped again, leaving a few freshly cut hairs stuck to the sweat on my neck.

"Don't squirm, Dough."

I guess, watching these other women, and then looking at my mother, I began to think she was okay, even pretty, not pretty like

Val but pretty like a mother ought to be, like the Virgin Mary or a mom you might see on TV. She had her black hair nearly cut to her shoulders in a nice bob and she never wore any tight pants or anything embarrassing like that. Most of the time, she was quiet and gentle the way you'd want your mother to act, but sometimes she'd just surprise the hell out of you. I glanced at her in the mirror as she worked on the hair around my left ear, and then the shiny silver door to the beauty salon flashed open, slamming against the frame. Mr. Darve strode in, scaring the whole parlor with the look in his blackened eyes. He wore a blue-and-gray work shirt from his job at the service station. His hair was greasy and black and stood up in the back. His face was all whiskered and red and hard, a look I had seen on a number of my mother's boyfriends.

"Okay, I'm just gonna ask once. Where is it, Dolores?" He strode right up to his wife and gripped her by her wrist. Mrs. Darve's smudged eyebrows seemed to tremble. "Let's not argue. Just tell me where you put it." He shook her hard, snapping her head back and forth on her thin shoulders.

"It's gone," she mumbled, trying not to cry, but the tears were already there. "It's all gone. I poured it out this morning."

Mrs. Larue snapped to her feet and forced herself between Mr. Darve and his wife, inching her wide hips in front of him. I looked over at the commotion as my mother stopped trimming my hair.

"Just a minute, Eddie, you aren't bursting into my store and starting some trouble."

"Can it, Edna. This is between me and my wife."

"No," my mother muttered. "This is Edna's place. You can't just come in here drunk and start trouble."

Mr. Darve shot my mother a cold, mean look, still gripping his wife by her wrist. "I just want to know what you did with my liquor," he whispered, turning to his wife again. The deacon's fat wife, Mrs. Heget, backed away, standing in the shadow of the bulbous hair dryer.

"You let go of her, Eddie," Mrs. Larue warned, "before I call the police."

"You call the police. 'Cause doing what she did is a crime too."

"She didn't do anything wrong," my mother said, her hands on her hips. "All she did was pour it out."

"Is that right? You really poured it out?" Mr. Darve asked. Tiny blue streams of tears ran down Mrs. Darve's face as she nodded. "Why did you do that, honey?"

"I told you. I was scared."

"You're gonna pay me back for what you poured out. Do you understand?"

Her blue eyelids flickered with tears. "Yes."

"Good." He let go of her wrist. "Go get your purse. I'll take what you got now."

Mrs. Darve trembled to her feet and ran into the back of the store, sobbing. Mrs. Larue followed, pushing open the tiny pink curtain and disappearing into the back room. Mr. Darve's face was bright red. He sneered at my mother, holding his hands on his hips like a proud fool. Looking at him, I felt a hard black knot in my stomach.

When Mrs. Larue returned to the room, she was holding her hands behind her back.

"Well, where the hell is she?" Mr. Darve asked.

I could not believe my eyes. In Mrs. Larue's hand was a small, shiny .22, powerful enough to blow a hole right through Mr. Darve's skull.

"Don't move," Mrs. Larue warned, sticking the muzzle right against his chin. "Don't move or Dolores is going to be a widow."

Mr. Darve let out a little squeak.

"It's okay, Dolores. Come on out," Mrs. Larue said quietly. "Come on out." Mrs. Darve appeared from the back room, holding herself. Her face was red and puffy from crying. She stepped in front of her husband, staring at his face.

"Now you tell this poor woman you love her. Go ahead. Tell her, you bum!" Mrs. Larue shouted.

"I love you," Mr. Darve said, squinting hard.

"Tell her she is the only one for you," Mrs. Larue muttered.

"You're the only one for me."

"Tell her you're sorry for ruining her life by making her cry all the time!" the preacher's wife shouted.

"I am sorry for ruining your life by making you cry all the time."

"Now kiss her hand," Mrs. Larue said with a smile.

Mr. Darve reached out and kissed his wife's hand. Mrs. Larue jabbed him in the eye with the muzzle, backing him toward the door.

"If you ever lay a hand on poor Dolores again, I swear to God, the last thing you hear will be me laughing, just before I pull this trigger." Mrs. Larue shoved the gun hard against his cheek. "Now go home and sleep it off."

Mr. Darve shot out of the beauty salon and into the street, holding his eye, mumbling to himself. All the ladies let out a breath, Mrs. Darve still crying. Me, I let out a breath too. My mother untied the apron around my neck, squatted beside me, and said, "Tell French it looks like I'll be home late, okay?" She reached into her jeans and handed me a dollar.

As I was running out, Mrs. Heget stopped me, touching my shoulder, and said, "We hope to see you again this Sunday, Dough. We missed you last week. Sunday school just isn't the same without you and your brother."

I didn't utter a word, just nodded.

"Oh, they'll be there," my mom said, patting me on the head. She leaned beside me and whispered, "Stay out of trouble, okay?"

"Okay," I said, and ran toward the filling station as fast as I could, wondering what I could blow a dollar on, not wanting to think about having to go back to Sunday school.

Every week Pill and I were supposed to go to Sunday school on account of the both us never being baptized, because at the time our parents weren't much concerned with things like church. I guess my father dying and the thought of his soul being lost in Purgatory was something I didn't want to think about. For me, Sunday school was a horror show, the worse way to spend a week-end afternoon. Most of the time we are able to ditch, except when my mom and French went to church, which, thank God, was never that often. Sunday school was held in a tiny classroom in a part of a building that was a recent addition to the church; the roof was sheet metal and it looked like the walls were made of tin.

"What do you mean, kissing is a sin?" Elroy Viceroy shouted. He was fourteen with all kinds of red pimples across his face. He always tried to be a real smart-ass during Bible Class. "That isn't one of the Commandments."

Mrs. Heget smiled. Her round face blushed. Every Sunday she'd try to get a bunch of teenagers and middle-schoolers to understand the true nature of the human spirit, helping us to con-template God's unconditional love, but it wasn't easy. No one in the class wanted to be there. I knew I'd rather be asleep or at home watching motorcross or out running around with some matches or trying to teach that dumb dog Shilo how to kill.

"First of all, kissing before marriage can lead to sex and mas-turbation. And well, sex is sex. And masturbation is not proper behavior for a growing boy. It could lead to damage and injury and even night blindness."

Mrs. Heget tolerated our lack of enthusiasm to a certain degree. She was polite and calm and was always telling us what we were and weren't supposed to do and think and say. Heck, I was eleven. I was having a dirty thought every other minute. Jesus seemed nice to me, so did the rest of all the saints, but I guess I didn't understand anything more than that.

"Night blindness?" Elroy muttered. "How long does it take before you go blind?"

"Not very long." Mrs. Heget frowned. "It is a sin and something you will either have to confess or pay for in the afterlife. Any other questions about Purgatory?"

"I got one," I said, raising my hand.

"Yes, Dough," she answered with a smile, crossing her wide white legs beneath her billowy dress.

"If you're a good person, right, and you commit some sins, but mostly you're good, do go to hell or not?"

Pill rolled his eyes at the desk beside mine. He shook his head and resumed staring at the back of Lula Getty's neck.

"Well, Dough, that is an interesting question." Her round face stiffened as she figured up an answer. "I think if you're basically a good person, and you've accepted Jesus into your life, well, I think then God would surely find a place for you in heaven."

"Okay, well, what if you were basically a good person and committed a crime during your life?"

"What kind of crime?"

"I dunno. Stealing stuff."

Her face tightened even more.

"I think if you're truly sorry, then God will forgive you. God will always forgive you. He cared so much about all of you to send his only son to die for your sins. He'd forgive you as long as you really wanted to be forgiven." She took a breath and nodded to herself. "Any other questions?"

"Okay, so what if you die in the middle of a crime? Like you're robbing a bank or something, then you get shot."

"You're probably going to hell then." Her answer was very curt.

I nodded, unhappy with her answer. Who else was I going to ask? It didn't seem to bother Pill. And as for my mother, who was sometimes so filled with the Holy Ghost that it kept her up at night, praying for all of us, well, I guess I was afraid that if I ever asked her about my dad, she'd just begin sobbing and wouldn't ever stop.

I raised my hand once again. "Well, what about Purgatory and all that? Doesn't that count?"

She let out a little sigh, trying to gather herself. She made a little smile and stared at me.

"Like I said, Dough, if the person truly wants to be forgiven, then God willing, they will be forgiven and granted a place in heaven."

I thought that sounded better. Maybe there was some hope for me and my brother after all.

"Does anyone else have any other questions now?"

I looked around the room and saw that the whole tiny classroom was silent. I turned to my brother who was staring at Lula Getty's neck. You couldn't help but think dirty thoughts when you looked at that girl. She seemed very bored with everything and I noticed that she was wearing a gold pendant around her neck in the shape of a wolf. About a week before, I had seen her walking home, smoking, with her right hand bent at the wrist, gossiping about something with some other girl, their red lipstick like wounds on their lips. Of course, then a black Camaro drove by, braking to a dusty stop, and Rudy LaDell got out and hollered a thing or two and Lula swore something back. Eventually, she just shrugged her shoulders and hopped into the car and they just sped away, down the old gray road beside the culvert near our trailer park. I decided to follow and it was there, where the apple orchard started, that I saw the two of them necking, her long fifteen-year-old legs flung apart, rocking the car as I watched from down in the culvert, shaking my head.

I thought this girl, Lula, was as lost as me or my brother. I glanced back at him, his eyes were full of hopelessness and he was making little kisses with his mouth, dreaming of Lula's lips.

"Pill? Are you all right?" Mrs. Heget asked. Pill snapped awake. He sat straight up and knocked the silver-bound Bible to the floor and then rubbed the side of his face. Everyone in Bible class looked at him and laughed. Lula turned around and shook her head. Her curly red hair hung over her face as she shot my brother a dirty look.

"Creep," she mumbled.

He reached over and picked up the Bible and started staring at the back of her neck again.

After about an hour of Mrs. Heget's talking about Jesus, the class would end with Sunday service in the gray pews of Our Queen of Holy Martyrs Church. I'd spend most of the service staring up at Jesus nailed to the wood cross. Through the kneeling and praying, all I would think about was my dad and his funeral, and how cold and gray his casket had looked, how the flowers had dried up because of the heat, and how my mother had cried all day until someone gave her some Valium to fall asleep. I would remember how my fat Aunt Marie had wailed as they heaved the coffin out of the church and that forever kind of sound of the box disappearing down, down, down into that shallow bed of dirt. All those kind of memories would make me feel about as unwelcome in church as anything could. I'd walk home beside Pill, wondering how much of what we had just been told was true, or if like my older brother said, it was just some other lie I had fallen for.

* * *

That day I came home from service and stopped outside my new neighbor's recently erected white picket fence. It surrounded the front of his trailer, making it seem more like a home, which I thought looked nice. My brother had gone to the filling station to try to pick up some smokes so I stood alone beside Mr. del Perdito's fence and watched as he painted the last remaining slats. I decided I had to say something to him if I ever wanted to try and sleep again.

"Hey, you live here, right?" I grunted, staring at his bare olive-colored chest. There was a tattoo of a brilliant green snake wrapped around his upper left arm and another one of an angel praying just below the opposite shoulder.

"Yes, sir. My name is El Rey del Perdito. What can I do for you, my friend?"

I got right to the point: "Do you think you can cut that noise out at night?"

"Pardon?" the old man said. He stared at me, a little shocked by my lack of politeness. He rubbed some sweat from his face with a small white towel.

"All that music. It's driving my mother crazy."

"Oh, *lo siento, perdoname*. I am sorry. I didn't think anyone minded my dancing. Let us talk about it over a cold soda, shall we?"

"I guess."

"What's your name, sir?"

"Dough."

"Very wonderful name, my friend. Let us retire to the mansion, Dough, to secure some soda, eh?"

"All right."

He opened up the screen door and held it for me as I stepped inside. El Rey's motor home was mostly empty. There was a small record player in one corner, a cardboard box full of records beside it, an old gray refrigerator at the opposite end of the place, some pillows and blankets thrown in the middle of the floor. El Rey opened up the refrigerator and pulled out a cold can of soda and placed it in my hand.

"Hey, who's that?" I asked. There was a black-and-white picture of a dark-eyed woman with long hair that was decorated with a number of jeweled combs. The photo sat right on the floor beside the old man's makeshift bed. In it, the woman's dress was a tight corset, sparkling with more jewels around her shoulders. I picked up the picture and stared at her round face.

"That was my wife. Dolcita. The Tango Queen of Santa Ana," he said, staring up at the ceiling. "Her feet were hummingbird wings. The way she moved when she danced, it was like flying."

El Rey made a little dance move, holding one hand to his hips, while his other gripped the hand of some imaginary dance partner. He began to turn in time to the rhythm in his head. *"Da-da-da, da-da-da."* He turned and stopped and stared down at me.

"She died last April. Cancer. In her stomach. There was nothing we could do to save her." He stared down at the picture and smiled. "Sometimes I feel like I am caught in the worst nightmare of my entire life and there's no way to escape it. Sometimes I think I don't ever want to sleep again. Did you ever lay in your bed too scared to fall asleep? You feel like the whole world is on your head and you'll never be able to rest again?"

I shrugged my shoulders and then nodded.

"That's the time I dance, my friend. That's the perfect time right there." He strode over to the tiny black-and-gold record player and pulled a record from its sleeve, then set it in place. He dropped the black arm and needle into the proper plastic groove. "That is the best time in the world to let all that agony out right through your feet."

The tango music boomed on. His bare gray chest began to get sweaty as he moved.

"C'mon, Dough, dance. Dance with me, no?"

He grabbed my hand and set me into motion, swinging me about. He was old and thin but still kind of strong. He danced beside me, then spun me across the room.

"That's it, my friend. Now you've got it. This is the only way to keep her alive. The dance!" he shouted over the music. He gave a little hop, then did a quick turn and bowed just as the music ended. He held his position and blew a kiss to an imaginary audience. "Bravo!" he shouted, taking another bow. He picked up the tiny white towel and began to wipe his forehead and bare chest. *"Bien. Muy bien.* You're well on your way to becoming a great dancer."

He patted me on the back.

"Hey, listen, Mr. Rey, I was wondering, well, do you think you can cut that music out at night? My mother . . ."

"Yes?"

"It's just too noisy for her."

He studied my face and then said, "I see. Well, I will do my best to keep it down. How is that?"

I nodded, looking around the empty trailer.

"Well, I must go and finish my fence. And also I must practice the cha-cha-cha. If you don't practice, you forget everything, I'm afraid." El Rey closed the door behind me and I cringed as I heard the needle strike the record, the sound of the cha-cha-cha reverberating from within the empty motor home.

I opened up the screen door and stepped inside our own trailer. My mother and French were at the kitchen table with the old lady that lived in the lot behind us, Mrs. Garnier. She was the one who lived with at least three million cats, all of them ugly, underfed, scrawny animals with rotten faces and worms that bled from their rectums, cats that scratched at her screen door all night and hissed and left dead birds on her front door and fought each other in the gray gravel dirt of the trailer park. I guess Shilo had nearly torn one of those cats apart a few weeks before, catching the poor thing in its gray jaws before me and my brother could pull the damn thing loose. Shilo had pulled a hunk of fur and skin from its mangy neck. When it happened, Mrs. Garnier had come stomping over, threatening to sue unless we kept poor Shilo chained up. That dumb dog was not happy about sitting at the end of a length of chain. But now the dog hopped around in front of the trailer during the day on his three legs howling and snarling like a deformed puppet because there was nothing else we could do.

I looked over at my mother, who smiled at me as I slumped onto the sofa. Shilo came up and dropped his head into my lap. Mrs. Garnier had a piece of paper all knotted up in her gray fists and was talking so excitedly that it was hard to understand what she was saying.

"It's indecent is what I think," Mrs. Garnier said with a frown. "An old man acting like that, it's indecent. There's children running around all night and day, what would happen if they saw what was going on over there?"

About a month before, Mrs. Garnier had caught me and my brother smashing bluebird eggs against the side of our trailer. They were from a nest we had found in a small tree in the field behind the trailer park. She had grabbed me by my ear and my brother by his hair and led us around the front of our trailer and told our mother exactly what we'd been doing. "Heathens!" is what she had called us. "Heathens!" Of course, I had seen at least a thousand of her cats murder, maim, and mutilate a million robins, sparrows, cardinals, any unlucky bird that landed anywhere near the shadow of that old lady's trailer. Once, I had even seen two or three of her cats tear a rabbit apart, strewing its remains all across her front steps. Before El Rey had moved in next door, the only sound at night would be the awful scream of her cats killing poor woodland creatures.

"Now wait a minute." My mother frowned. "No one said you had to watch what that man does at night. You can just close your curtains if you want."

"What about the noise? That horrible music blaring. Him banging around all night. It's inconsiderate, to say the least. Don't you agree?" Mrs. Garnier turned to French this time for support.

"I guess," he said. His face was long. It looked like the old lady was wearing him out.

"I'm an old woman, and all I have left is my sleep. We pay too much to live in this park to be disturbed by someone so inconsiderate. When it comes down to it, it's a question of morals. I'm sure you wouldn't want your boys to see the things going on over there, would you?"

"No," my mother said. "But—"

"But nothing. Are you going to sign the petition or not?"

"No, I don't think so," my mother said with a frown.

"It's a shame your boys don't have better role models to look up to. Bad apples don't fall far from the tree."

"Good day, Mrs. Garnier," my mother announced, opening the screen door for her.

"Hmphh," the old lady grunted, wobbling down the front steps.

French shook his head, taking a swig from his silver can of beer.

"Who does that old bag think she is to go around bothering people like that?" my mother asked.

"Doesn't look like it matters. There were enough names on that petition without us." He sat the beer can down and stared out the kitchen window. Mrs. Garnier pounded on El Rey's screen just once, then slipped the petition between the door and the frame and waddled away.

"I guess I'll go work on the car," French said. I didn't think that his black Impala was ever going to get off those four concrete blocks. He opened another can of cold beer and patted me on the back. "Feel like giving me a hand there, pal?"

I saw my mother smiling at me hopefully.

"I guess," I grunted, digging my fists into my pockets. French pulled the rest of his six-pack out of the fridge and stepped outside. I followed, helping him yank the dirty white tarp off the useless black car. We folded it between the two of us and set it down beside the rear blocks.

There it was. Oh, '72 Impala. What a waste. Even the red rust on the wheel wells looked like it had given up hope. We stood there before it, me shaking my head with a frown, French grinning, patting his belly.

"She's a real beauty, isn't she?" French sighed, taking a sip of beer. "Let's see if she'll turn over." He propped open the driver's door. Turn over? Turn over? That car had never once started before. I leaned against the side of it, shaking my goddamn head.

French slid the silver key into the ignition, closed his eyes, and gave the ignition a quick turn. I don't know how, but there was a sputter somewhere deep inside. Ol' French gave it another mean crank.

"Give up," I mumbled, as French let out a sigh and leaned back in the lush vinyl seat, then took a swig from his silver can.

"Doesn't look like it's our day, does it, pal?"

He finished off the beer and crushed the can in one hand, which seemed kind of impressive to me. He yanked another can off the plastic ring and tapped the top three times, staring at me with a wide grin.

"You ever split a beer with your old man?" he asked.

I suddenly felt embarrassed for some reason. I don't why. I guess I just didn't like him mentioning my dad.

"Do you feel like tasting a sip?"

I stared at him hard and shook my head.

"C'mon, it'll put a little hair on your chest."

I shook my head again and spat into the dirt. French shrugged his shoulders and heaved himself out of the car, then propped up the hood and started poking about. I leaned against the back of the car, staring over at El Rey's mobile home, watching as the old man hunched over, applying a second coat of paint to his new picket fence. There was sweat all along his bare chest and back. His face looked happy as he moved the thick black brush over the slats of wood, singing to himself some tango or cha-cha-cha. I smiled to myself, then turned and watched French tear out some slinky mechanical device from under the hood.

"Here's our problem all right." French smiled through a face full of grease. I shook my head and turned back to watch El Rey running the brush against the wood. His greasy pompadour seemed to glow. Just then, a tall man walked up to the white fence, staring down at El Rey with a frown.

"Yer the man that lives here then?" the tall man asked. His voice was loud and sounded angry. There was a glare off the tall man's large forehead. He wore a dark blue pair of overalls and had a wide frown on his face. It was Mr. Deebs, the man who worked at the cemetery, the man from the trailer two lots down. He was the person who dug the ditch they dropped you in when you were a goner. He lived alone in a blue trailer, just on the other side of the tiny gravel road. I did not like the looks of him. He used to stand behind his screen door, cleaning his gun, while he watched me and my brother sitting behind our trailer smoking our cigarettes or shooting the bull. He'd just stand there behind his screen with a thin little smile, swabbing out his rifle's firing mechanism, maybe wondering exactly how long it might take to entirely dissect me and my brother limb from limb.

"I come here to ask you when you plan on leaving."

I watched El Rey as he put down his paintbrush and smiled. He wiped some white enamel on his pants and stood up. Mr. Deebs just kept frowning, tightening his fists.

"I said, when do you plan on leaving?"

"I don't think I understand." El Rey grinned. "I just moved in. I just put up this fence. I don't plan on leaving for some time, my friend."

"I don't think you understand what I mean."

"No, I think I do."

"Well, you might consider being gone real soon is all I'm gonna say."

"I am going to have to ask you to please leave now."

Mr. Deebs clenched his jaw and shifted his weight, tightening his shoulders in place. He twitched his lips a little, then looked down at the tiny white fence. "I don't think I will," he said.

I looked back and saw that French was watching what was happening too, from around the hood of the Impala. "You all right over there?" French called out.

"Yes, yes," old El Rey replied. His face looked tired and gray.

French set down his wrench and grabbed an oily rag, wiping off his hands. He strolled slowly over to El Rey's fence, nodding with a big smile.

"Is there something I can help you with?" he asked Mr. Deebs.

"Nope. It ain't got nothing to do with you," the tall man answered.

"I think it might be a good idea if you go on back home there, pal," French said, and then, misjudging the situation, he reached up and put his hand on Mr. Deebs's shoulder. From where I was standing, I saw at once it was the wrong thing to do. Mr. Deebs knocked French's hand off his shoulder and then gave him a shove. French was still smiling, lifting his hands up, trying to make it clear that he didn't want any trouble, but Mr. Deebs took a wild swing, catching French in the corner of his left eye with a sharp knuckle.

At that point, French stopped smiling and lunged forward, wrapping his arm around the other man's neck, wrestling him to the ground, getting him in a headlock.

"Go on, be still!" French shouted. "Be still." He kept squeezing hard until Mr. Deebs gave in and just laid there, kicking his foot in little circles. "Don't come around here again, do you understand? We don't want trouble, okay? Stay on your side of the road and we won't have any more of this."

Breathing hard, Mr. Deebs grunted something through the dust. French let him up, and the thin man took off down the little street, back into his blue trailer, leaving some of his pride there outside El Rey's house.

"You okay?" French asked El Rey.

The old man smiled, his face wrinkled with worry. "I'm going to go inside now. It's too much for me." His face looked empty and old. The tattoos on his arms suddenly seemed dull, the grace in his step gone.

"I think that's maybe a good idea," French said. He turned, holding his shoulder, and looked me right in the face. Me, I didn't move. I didn't say a word.

He kind of stumbled toward our trailer, clenching his shoulder and gritting his teeth. "C'mere," he whispered, tightening his face in pain. I wiped the sweat off my forehead and wandered over to where he stood in front of our trailer door. His long thin face was covered in sweat too. His eyes were small and dull like was about to fall asleep.

"Be a sport and go get me my beer."

I ran over and pulled the rest of the six-pack off the roof of the black car and placed the plastic ring in his hand. He sat down on our porch with a groan, then took the four cold metal cans and placed them against his neck, rubbing his shoulder with a frown.

"I think I threw out my shoulder. Jesus."

I stared at him, watching as his left eye began to swell up.

"Don't think this is the way you're supposed to handle things, pal," French mumbled, wiping some blood from his neck with the palm of his hand. "Because it's not. You should always try to talk things out. But sometimes it's not so easy. Sometimes, well, people won't let you talk, but you got to try at least."

French was still breathing hard. I guess he was as stunned as me.

"Let's go inside now and tell your mother what happened." He stood and spat hard into the gravel. That was maybe the first time I realized that he wasn't planning on skipping out on us anytime soon. I mean, he put up with me and my crazy brother and my mother crying by herself at night. He was in for the long haul, and maybe the best thing I could do was just get used to it.

I opened up the screen door for him, watching as he stumbled inside. My mother was on the sofa and turned to smile, but then caught sight of French's swollen eye.

"June," he mumbled. "Don't get excited. But there was some sort of fight."

"What happened to your eye?"

Of course, my mother broke into tears right away, hurrying to get some ice to put on his face. French let out a little groan as he took a seat on the couch, adding a little sigh for some sympathy. And sure enough, that night I heard my mother laughing, the sound of them doing it echoing through the walls and their bedroom door.

* * *

After school the very next day, El Rey's mobile home was gone.

And no one said a word about it.

For about a week after he left, I stared out the window at night to try to see if he maybe might come back. I pushed the red curtains aside and pressed my nose against the dirty glass. But he had really disappeared. His mobile home was gone. The echo of his records, of his singing, had vanished too. It was as if he had never been there at all. I laid in bed and wondered what happens to people when they go, if they become like shadows, if they fade away when they disappear from your life. The only thing I could see was the broken picket fence. The only sound I could hear was the cry of birds being killed in the night.

the devil lives in texas

On that Halloween, which was the worst Halloween ever, because I dressed up as the Wolfman and Pill refused to dress up at all, my mother and French let us watch *The Texas Chain Saw Massacre,* and about a day or so later I started wetting the bed like a little cry-baby. It happened almost every night afterwards. In the morning, my brother would look at me and shake his head, then my mom would come in and pull off the sheets, trying not to look embarrassed for me. What I had been afraid of at first, leopards and tigers, had become something different in my dreams, something so frightening that I'd wet myself before I could even wake up. It was the Devil, the one I had seen in that lonely barn; he would appear in my dreams every night and my father would be there too. They would both meet somewhere on a lonely road in Texas, one black strip of tar, brilliant with blue and gray stones, the whispers of wild animals growling in the dark. There was no beginning to my dream. There was only an end.

Shadows would surround my old man, three of them. My dad would turn to face them, unafraid to meet his maker, which was the way he was, and then they'd come down on him with their crowbars and knives.

CRACK!

One of them would catch my dad under his chin with a crow-bar, knocking his teeth straight up into his head. My old man would be a lumped shadow on the black ground. Everything would turn to blood under his hands, sticky and hot like the tar. Behind him would be the square shadows of his idling truck and trailer. Night would be like an axe upon his head. He would glance up, trapped, and I would somehow see his face, but he would try to get me to look away. My old man would yank his short knife from his belt, leaning against one of the cold rubber wheels.

The three shadows would circle around him. Three of them. Three black shadows like crows. My dad would lunge and cut one down, cleaving the knife through one of their hands, sawing three full fingers straight off. The fingers would land in a perfect circle of blood with three drops each. The black blood would soak into the ground and vanish. The three fingers would then become white worms and crawl away. The wounded one would stand without any pain. They were not men. They were spooks or ghosts or Devils or whatever you want to call them. My dad would see he was fighting ghosts and would then nod, gritting his teeth. *"Let's go!"* my old man would shout, unafraid. *"Let's go!"*

One of them would catch him with the crowbar again, poking him in his belly.

Breathe, Dad, breathe.

He'd let out a grunt, clutching his guts, trying to strike at them with his knife, but his pain would be too much. His belly would tighten as he'd heave to the ground. He would cry out and his teeth would be knocked loose again by another blow. He'd begin to cry, realizing it was the Devil who had finally come for his soul. There'd be sharp-eyed angels with knife-edged wings floating in a halo around my old man's head. The three shadows would draw tighter and tighter around him. He would howl, trying to fight. The knife would slide through his bloody fingers, dropping from his hands. *Breathe, Pops, breathe.* He would cough, feeling a shaft of light burning along his spine. The three shadows would pull the silver cab keys from my old man's front pocket. He would coil like a dead snake at their feet. He would be shivering so bad. He wouldn't be able to move. His black cowboy hat would blow off his head, disappearing into the night. *Depart from me, ye cursed, into the fire prepared for the Devil and his angels.*

He would gurgle up more blood, trying to curse. Then they would steal his heart next. They would lean over and take his soul. The Devil would appear suddenly, a shadow twisted into a shape, spiraling into a single dark form on this road in Texas. In my dreams, the Devil would be the same awful creature I had seen in the haunted barn, a tall man with the head of a hooded lizard, a monster who wore a shimmering cloak of red, dripping with blood. The Devil's spiny mouth would open just before he set his tiny teeth into my old man's chest. My old man was going to hell. His ventricles would pump out fire. His teeth would turn to dust and disappear into the highway gravel. His skull would become a stone in the pavement road. His ghost would fold in a flash of sulfur, leaving a little black mark in the dirt.

I'd wake up too late then, feeling the awful wetness between my legs. I'd lie there, or try to go back to sleep, not wanting to wake my brother, not wanting to be teased, or worse, not wanting anyone to be ashamed of me. I would lie there, shivering a little, wondering if my dad, in heaven or hell or wherever he was, wanted to talk to me as bad as I wanted to talk to him.

I guess, as my brother explained it, my old man had been a highwayman. His name had been Lou. Everyone called him Lucky. Even my mom. His face was thin with some whiskers and his eyes were bright blue and kind of sad. There was a long scar that hooked from the corner of his lip around to the corner of his eye. He had a different story every time you asked him about that scar. By the time I was born, he was a trucker, the owner and operator of his own rig. Pill said he sometimes smuggled stolen cigarettes. I always thought of him as a cowboy and the happiest per-

son I think I ever knew. They found his body beneath the big black
wheels of his eighteen-wheeler somewhere on a nowhere road in
East Texas. I was seven at the time. Pill was ten. They wouldn't let
me or Pill see the body when they brought it back up by rail. But
me and my brother listened to every word my mother said, weeping on the telephone to her friends and family. Pill said he overheard
exactly what had happened to my dad. That's the benefit of an older
brother, though I still don't know how much of it was true, I guess.

After his death, my brother and I decided that my dad had
lost his soul in some sort of deal gone wrong. Maybe it sounds stupid to you, but like I said, I was only seven at the time, and when
they shipped my dad home in a mahogany box like some sort of
present, it made more sense than anything else anyone had been
telling me. Even at that age, I knew my old man had been a troublemaker, just like me and my brother, and I guess I figured that
he had gotten himself into trouble with the law, or maybe with the
people who hired him to run the stolen cigarettes from town to
town, or with someone else. We kind of made up the story that he
had sold his soul, and down there in Texas is where the Devil had
decided to collect. I do know that my mother had been very reli-
gious, even before my old man got killed, and I guess I was afraid
that a spook or maybe even his ghost might try to visit us after he
died, but she had this beautiful statue of the Virgin Mary which she
placed on my nightstand and I was able to sleep without any trouble after that. The Virgin was folding her hands in prayer, all silver
and white and gold, with a crack right along her throat, from where
I dropped her. I loved that statue. Her feet were bare and treading
right over a snake; a barefoot lady standing on a snake like that, so
calm and sweet. I was sure a powerful thing like that would scare
off any kind of evil, but it broke when we moved to the trailer park,
and by then I was convinced that my father had really been taken
by the Devil, and me and my lousy brother were sure to go next.

* * *

Ol' Pill didn't like talking about our dad that much.

He'd rather talk about girls.

We used to go down to the culvert every day after school. We'd smoke cigarettes and look at dirty magazines and just sit there and talk or not talk at all. Every few hundred feet there was a silver pipe that leaked green sewage down into the small stream. We'd go sit on one of the pipes, right along this real steep gorge where brown sticker bushes and small trees grew. There were blue racer snakes and stick bugs and things like that, but mostly we just went there to get away from the goddamn trailer park, because when your home is so tiny, there isn't anywhere to go to do some thinking but in your room or the bathroom, and you can only spend so much time in either place before you start going a little crazy.

I'd stare at my brother until he'd pass me a Marlboro and then I'd choke on it as he'd light it. I'd let the smoke charge down my lungs until I thought I was going to die, then I'd try to puff it out real smooth and cool, but it always came out in a cough. Pill would just laugh, shaking his head, not doing much better himself.

"Did you make it with a girl yet?" I asked him one day. I felt like it was my duty as his younger brother to keep on top of those things. To be honest, I had no way to know if what he told me was ever the truth or not.

"Nope." He said this like it really hurt him. His eyes got real thin and black and he stared down into the green creek like he was thinking something so heavy that there was no way he could manage to keep his head up. "But I'll tell you about the time I fingered Gretchen Hollis."

He took a long drag, fighting to keep himself from coughing.

"We were at her pool party last spring and everyone had gone on home so there was just three of us—me and Gretchen and Bobby Shucksaw—but he had to go on because his sister had a baseball game, and so then it was just me and Gretchen sitting there all alone drying off."

I had heard this story at least a million times, and every time, every time, it made my palms sweat and my head feel light.

"So it's just me and Gretchen. Then she goes: 'Do you wanna make out?' And I go, 'Yep.'"

Now, you might think my brother was making something like that up, but I knew Gretchen Hollis. She was pretty and round-headed with yellow hair. She was the first girl I knew in my old neighborhood in Duluth who got a hickie. Her mother almost beat the hell out of her for it and sent her to school with a black eye not far from the red love-mark on the side of her neck.

"So we start making out."

"What's that like?" I asked.

My brother shook his head, like I was a total amateur.

"Listen, I'm telling a goddamn story here, you can't keep butting in with your stupid questions, okay?"

He rubbed out the half-smoked cigarette and lit up another, coughing up great plumes of smoke.

"So we're making out and Gretchen has on a two-piece and I decide to go for second base." He accentuated this last remark by gripping the air with both hands, giving a good squeeze with all his fingers. "So by now we're in the garage, right behind their car, and we're still making out and I got my hand up her top and then I hear her old man hollering from her back porch."

I used to think that her dad was a goddamn monster. He had a square jaw and plenty of whiskers and once I'd seen him kick a dog that wasn't even his.

"And her dad keeps calling for her and by then I had both my hands up her top and she was still trying to kiss me and I was start-ing to get scared. I could hear her old man out on the porch look-ing around and so I try to stop. But she won't stop kissing me."

That's the part of the story I always had trouble believing, but it was Pill's story so I kept it to myself.

"Then I can see Mr. Hollis's shadow, he's standing right in front of the goddamn car, hollering and cussing, and poor Gretchen is trembling in my arms and my hands are all stuck up her top and I'm worried as hell too, but I can't make a move and I feel his shadow pass right over us and he goes back in the house."

He let out a breath like he hadn't breathed all day, shaking his head with a horrible grin.

"That's when she told me she wanted me to do it with her, right there."

I would imagine Gretchen Hollis's tiny lips as they made those words over and over again in my head.

Do it with me.

Do it with me.

Do it with me.

I would imagine her eyes as silver as stars and her perfectly round head. In my fantasy, her curly blond hair stank of chlorine. I would imagine her tiny white fingers locking with my brother's, showing where she had bit her fingernails. Every time I heard that story I'd feel my stomach tighten and my palms get greasy whenever he got to that part. A girl in her garage, half-naked, smelling like chlorine, and the words, *Do it with me,* I guess that always seemed like a moment of endless possibilities.

My brother flicked his dying cigarette into the green creek and looked away to finish his story.

"But I didn't wanna get her pregnant or anything like that, so I just fingered her instead."

"What's that feel like?"

"I'm telling a goddamn story, if you don't mind."

He shook his head, staring down into the creek as a little paper cup floated by.

"Then she went in the house, and as I was leaving I heard her old man screaming and hollering and I took a goddamn brick and threw it against the side of their house and I shouted, 'I fucked Gretchen Hollis!' loud as I could."

His voice cracked a little at the end. He lit a few matches and tossed them down into the creek to watch them sizzle out. He had a look like he had just said too much maybe.

"God, I hate this fucking town. I wanna get the hell outta here."

He sounded helpless. I shrugged my shoulders.

"C'mon, we better get on over to Val's," I said.

He stood and stared down into the creek and then nodded.

I looked up and saw that the trees along the drainage ditch had become thin. Their leaves were clumped in tiny piles as we climbed along. There was the taste of burning wood in our teeth. Summer was over. Fall, unwelcome as it might have been, was already here.

When we got to Val's trailer, she looked awful, like a poor pink flower. She was trying on an ungodly chiffon bridesmaid's gown that she had been forced to buy for two hundred dollars. It looked gruesome. It was the color of peppermint antacid, the ugliest pink you could ever imagine. We crowded in her tiny bathroom, watching her as she turned, trying different poses, looking for one that didn't seem so awful. But no position worked. It was like the dress was haunted.

"It can't be as ugly as I think it is, can it, Dough? Pill?"

I didn't say a word, only shrugged my shoulders. Pill did the same. I guess her younger sister, Dottie, was getting married in a few weeks, which meant a few weeks of having to see Val trying it on over and over again.

"I hate to say it, but this is the most repulsive dress I've ever seen," Val muttered, turning once more before the full-length mirror. "I pray this is my sister's idea of some kind of bad joke."

I turned away, taking a seat on the edge of the tub, and that was when I saw it: *them*. I looked up and noticed Val's lacy black panties and brassiere drying along the shower curtain rod. I felt my heart pounding in my chest as I stared at them hanging there. Pill noticed them too, his face already turning red. He looked at them for a few moments, then hurried out of the bathroom to go sit on the porch and smoke a cigarette with his shaky hands.

"It feels like I'm wearing some sort of punishment," Val said. She turned and glanced over her shoulder at the monstrous pink bow that rippled at the base of her spine. "What in God's sweet name is that supposed to be?" The bow was huge, puffy, and knotted.

I sat on the edge of the tub, trying to smile, but my Val was right: It looked like some kind of pink curse.

"I look hideous. Hideous. I look like a hooker, don't I? I look like trailer trash."

And then Val began to cry. Sweet Jesus, help me, she began to cry. I didn't know what to say or do. I looked up at her, trying to smile.

"I guess it can't be that bad," she muttered, holding her hand over her mouth. And then she started crying even harder, sitting down on the bathroom floor, sobbing into the folds of her awful gown. "I look horrible. Horrible . . . like a . . ."

I watched as tears ran down her smooth white cheeks, turning the pink gown darker where her teardrops landed. I fought to think of some words I could use, something I could say that would make her stop crying, but nothing came. I guess Val did look horrible in that dress. I was afraid there were no words in the world that would change that. Somehow, dressed up in that chiffon gown, she did look cheap. I began to wonder if that was the way she always looked and maybe I had just never noticed. Under the fabric of that awful pink dress, the truth was now as bare and stunning as the black mole on her white shoulder. I began to think that maybe Val, with her dingy little job at the diner, and all her men, maybe she was exactly like the rest of us.

"I heard Mrs. Heget in the supermarket whispering to that Mrs. Groves," Val whispered. "She called me a tramp. She said, 'There goes that little whore!' I hate it here. I hate people thinking I'm a whore. Why can't I find a nice man? Why can't I meet someone who is nice to me for more than a week?"

I felt my teeth begin to ache as she kept on talking.

"I wish I could just pack up all my things and leave. Go somewhere where no one knows me. Where no one thinks bad things about me."

"I don't think bad things about you," I whispered.

"I know you don't, sweetie," she said. "I know." Her big black eyelashes flashed with tears and dripped mascara down her cheeks.

She pulled my hand to her face, holding it beside her lips. Then she kissed each finger, each of my fingers just once, still crying, still dripping makeup from her puffy pink eyes.

"I'm sorry, Dough. I'm sorry to make a fuss."

She kissed each of my knuckles and tried to smile, then pulled herself to her feet and began to take the dress off. Her fingers fought around behind her back.

"Do you think you can unzip me?"

I felt my heart stop and my mouth went dry. Both my ears felt red hot.

"Sure," I mumbled, trying not to collapse.

At the base of her back, above that ungodly pink bow, was a thin silver zipper. I held my breath and pulled the zipper to its lowest point, nearly fainting as the two folds of fabric fell open and showed the top of her bare behind.

"I'm going to take a bath," she said over her shoulder, holding the pink dress up against her naked flesh. I could honestly say that there, right there, more than anything in my life, I wanted to touch her and tell her all the things I thought I felt—that she was more beautiful than anyone or anything I had ever seen, that no dress could make her look cheap, that beneath it all there was a kind of beauty that no pink dress could ever disguise. But I guess I felt that saying those things would be a lie, and a lie that I didn't want to ever have to admit. I backed out of the bathroom, holding my fingers in a tight fist against my side.

I did not stare through the keyhole to watch Val take her bath. I did not try to marvel at the sight of her bare white thighs or shiny blond hair. I held my face against the fabric of her red velvet sofa, feeling lousy.

A little while later, my older brother went out and picked up a few bags of greasy fried chicken and we all sat down and ate, but I swear it was like nothing had a taste.

"Don't you like your fried chicken?" Val asked with a smile. Her blue eyes were still swollen from crying.

"I don't know, I'm not hungry tonight," I said with a frown. We all cleaned up the plates and silverware and set them in the sink. After dinner, it was time to sit out on the porch and tell jokes and take sips of Val's gin and soda, but for some reason I just couldn't look at the way she pretended to cross her eyes, making funny faces. I just didn't think it was so hilarious when she snorted a song through her nose. I thought all the jokes she told were corny and the way her hair was done up in a ponytail looked ugly. I finally decided to fake a stomachache and wander off to bed.

"Do you want some medicine?" Val asked, kissing my forehead so sweetly. "A cup of tea?"

"No thanks." I frowned and closed the spare bedroom door. I climbed into bed and held my fists to my eyes and felt like crying. I was sure they were both listening to hear if I was going to throw up or be sick. So I laid there quiet in her soft spare bed, watching the shadows on the wall making strange shapes.

Pill came in later, opening the bedroom door slowly to see if I was asleep. I looked him in his eyes and he shook his head to himself.

"You ain't really sick, are ya?" he asked, undressing in the dark.

"No, I'm okay."

"What's wrong with you?"

"It's that dress," I said.

"What's that supposed to mean?"

"I don't know."

I watched as my older brother settled into bed. We both waited there, under the covers, listening for some cowboy to arrive with flowers or wine. Beside my dumb older brother, there in the dark, lying in Val's soft white bed, I felt betrayed. I didn't even know why. It wasn't Val or that awful pink dress, really, not even the cowboy or the trucker who would soon arrive. I felt like I had been a dumb kid, thinking Val was better than the rest of us, when really she was just as doomed, just as lousy maybe. I pulled her soft comforter up over my head, mumbling to myself through her white pillows and sheets, hoping it was all a kind of dream I would somehow forget.

But then I couldn't sleep.

I held my breath and listened, waiting for one of her men to arrive. I heard the sound of a couple of big tires crunching against the gravel and then the mutter of an engine shutting off outside. I gritted my teeth, rolling on my stomach, staring at the way the headlights seemed to flicker then dim, in time to the beating of the blood in my head. I let go of my breath and waited for the knock, then the muffled laughter, then the silence, the silence which would be worse than anything.

There was the knock, the sound of knuckles against the door-frame.

But no reply.

No reply.

The knock came louder, a full-knuckled fist against the closed screen door. But there was no answer, no tiny laugh or any noise at all. I sat up in bed, staring at the bottom of the closed door. There were no lights on. The whole place was dark. I squinted a little as a third knock rattled the frame. There was no response, nothing, not a single sound.

I looked down at Pill. He was lying on his back, wide awake, listening to the silence too. "Maybe she's passed out," Pill muttered.

"Let's find out," I whispered, hopping out of the bed. My bare feet struck her cold tile floor. I opened the door slowly and stepped into that soft, lurid light.

I didn't hear anything in the darkness—no sounds, no movement, no drinks or records being played, no one laughing. By then the pickup outside and its driver had already begun to pull away. Pill and I stepped quietly across her trailer, staring at the soft lump on the couch. I could see, there in the darkness, her bare white toes. I smiled a little, holding my breath, listening to her sigh in her sleep. Her golden hair was shiny as her chest rose and fell. Her breasts moved with each breath. I could see something terrible in her arms. I could see she was not sleeping on the sofa alone. There she was, fast asleep, holding her white face to the billowy bridesmaid dress, right at the seam of that awful pink bow. I stood above her, watching as her eyes moved beneath their lids. A little snore whispered like a tiny bell. My hands began to ache. I don't know why, but I bent over and kissed one of her bare white toes. I held a breath in and started to creep back to bed, unable to keep the taste of her skin from swimming around in my head.

Pill just kept staring down at her with a frown, watching as her breasts rose and moved. He held his breath in his lungs tight, moving his hand over his eyes. Then he followed me back toward her spare room, but stopped at the bathroom door.

I could still see Val's precious underthings hanging there in the darkness. The dark blue light from outside shone upon the thin lace bra, showing the identical curves and gaps where it would lie against Val's skin. On that silver shower rod was an ungodly, awful mystery. I blinked as Pill stepped inside the bathroom and raised his hand to her black brassiere, touching the silk with one of his dirty fingertips. His face was red, his mouth dropped open, as he ran his fingers along its soft, smooth fabric. In a single beat, he turned and snatched it from its clothespins and shoved it under his shirt.

"The worse kind of person is a goddamn snitch," he warned, glaring at my dumbfounded stare. "Keep your damn mouth closed."

So I did.

We climbed back into her bed and I looked at him as he folded the black brassiere up tightly. His face looked long and mean. His eyes darted into mine and he sneered a little and laid back down onto bed. I didn't say a word about it. Not then, not ever. He was my older brother, he was my only older brother, and I was sure I would never say a word against him if I could. Maybe he had felt the same way, staring at Val all lonely and passed out on that red sofa, sleeping so close to that awful pink gown. Maybe seeing her asleep made him think she was just like us too, that she wasn't some far-off and mysterious thing, that she was just some other girl. He tucked her brassiere up under his shirt again and rolled over, turning away in the darkness with a snarl.

I shut my eyes and gave in to the darkness, letting myself fall into a deep, hollow sleep. I slept like the dead with no nightmares for the first time in a long while. I did not dream of my leopards or tigers. I didn't dream about my father or the Devil or anything.

Just before dawn, I woke up and found I had wet poor Val's bed.

I laid there under her white sheets, too embarrassed to move.

And so then I began to cry. I don't know why, but my eyes filled up with tears and my brother rolled over and woke up and shook his head when he saw my awful goddamn mess. My pajamas were soaked all the way through and so were parts of her nice white sheets.

"Don't tell her," I prayed to him. "Don't tell her, please."

His face was the worst look of disappointment I had ever seen. He cinched his lips together like he was about scream, but he didn't. He pointed at the foot of the bed and said: "Change into yesterday's clothes."

I nodded, still crying.

"Hurry up. And stop making so much damn noise crying like a little baby."

I nodded again and climbed out of the soiled bed. My face was hot with shame and my pants were all wet, and I was sure my Val was going to just happen to walk in while I was changing, but she didn't. I felt my heart beating hard in my throat until I had on my dry clothes from the day before. I stood staring at the stain on the one side of her square bed.

"What'll we do?" I kind of mumbled, trying not to sound terrified.

My brother let out a sigh. Quietly, he helped me strip the sheets off her bed and we sneaked it all out through her window and down into one of her garbage cans, then he helped me make the bed real nice.

After some breakfast, heck, Pill-Bug was the one who offered to take out the trash, and Val said, "That sure is nice," and he tossed it all out in the big metal dumpster five trailers away, not letting her know. I think it was then that I remembered why I was happy he was my older brother; he never told anyone, not a soul, that I was a bed-wetter, an eleven-year-old flat tire who cried in his sleep.

the star of silver is just plain lousy

About two months after we had moved to Tenderloin, Pill-Bug fell
in love with a knife. In the end, it would be the thing that finally
tore us apart, but of course neither one of us knew that, and to be
fair, I guess it wasn't just any stupid old knife. Really, the knife was
neat as hell: a brand-new Swiss Army Knife model 109, red and
trimmed in silver, with a miniature scissors, fork, spoon, saw, and
magnifying glass. They had taken Pill's other knife away a few days
after he set fire to Rudy LaDell's house. The principal had found
it in his locker, and even though my dad had been the one who
had given it to him, Pill had to wait until the end of the year to
get it back. This new knife, which we had come across at the hardware store, was some sort of weapon sent to him from God or the
Devil or both, whatever, it didn't really matter, it was meant for
him and him alone. It was kept behind a pane of smudged glass in
the hardware store, right beside the register, impossible to steal,
guarded by the clerk's steely gaze. But my brother and that knife
was just like every other love affair I ever came across, doomed,
unlucky, and sure not meant to be.

(People might say there ought to be some respect for the law and
its officials, and maybe there should be, but there's no way anyone
could respect a man like Deputy Lubbock, who would bust your
older brother's nose over a stupid knife, a knife that, paid for or
not, ought to have been his anyway.)

* * *

Thirty-six dollars: That's how much the knife cost. I didn't have thirty-six dollars. My brother didn't have thirty-six dollars. He didn't even have a job. Back in Duluth, he had been a paper boy and had lit our neighbor's hedge on fire the day before we left on account of the old bastard holding out on paying for his subscription. Pill had gotten stiffed out of twelve dollars, twelve dollars he was sure to never see again, twelve dollars that might have inched him a little closer to that knife. Heck, he was not about to get a job at the lousy Pig Pen, the supermarket where every other pimple-faced teenager in town worked, and so he devised a plan: "We're gonna steal that knife."

It was the dumbest thing I think I'd ever heard him say. But it was so full of hope that there was no way I could tell him any different. Which is how we first met Deputy Mort Lubbock.

Deputy Lubbock was an a-hole: There are some things you can tell about a person just by the way he looks. He was supposed to be handsome, in the way your mother or sister might call handsome, but for some reason, if you happened to see him, you knew he was a goddamn snake. I could see it in his smile. His smile was hard around the edges, like it was something he had practiced. He looked like he had spent a lot of time squinting and smiling at himself in a mirror in the dark, all alone in his lousy squad car, maybe listening to George Jones or Johnny Cash, looking in the rearview mirror like he was trying to convince himself of something. But there was nothing in that rearview mirror. I guess this deputy had a thing or two to hide, or that's what we heard. He had been an all-state linebacker back in high school, a real star, with scouts coming out to the games and making offers for scholarships, but this here deputy had lost it all just when that golden trophy had been so close and nearly right in his hands. I guess the deputy had knocked up a girl during his senior year of high school, a half-Chickasaw, half-white girl named Tiger-Lil, the daughter of a man who owned the town's only tow truck company. Apparently, under threat from his parents and hers, he married the girl, having to forget about going to state school and instead taking a lousy job in town as a tow truck operator for two years, until the baby was walking and his wife was settled in a nice duplex by the meat-packing plant. And then he got the phone girl at the towing service, Jurlene, knocked up. He planned to take her to Wisconsin for an abortion but she split town, without a forwarding address and with most of the tow truck service's cash. Those were probably the things that kept him looking in his rearview mirror all the time, a kind of desperate searching and waiting, a kind of squinting into the dark. There was something in his lousy face that showed his fear—no matter how many teeth he flashed, there was something waiting out there in the dark, hoping for the chance to catch up with him at last.

I guess the deputy sheriff was still something of a ladies' man. Rumor was that he would swing by other men's houses while they were hard at work at the meat-packing plant, up to their elbows in raw red flesh, heavy with sweat as they labored through the night, and this deputy would be sweaty and laboring through the night too, right in their soft, clean beds, right with their soft, clean wives, maybe searching for that lost sparkle somewhere between those ladies' thighs.

We would sometimes see him practicing shooting his revolver out near the haunted red barn, wearing a look on his face that warned us to keep our distance. He would smile like a snake, squeezing the trigger again and again, blowing holes through the wilted red boards. We would watch him and then stay away.

Besides deciding that he would to steal that prized knife, my brother didn't have any real plan. He wanted something, something he knew he'd never be able to afford on his own, and so he just decided that it should be his. I kind of thought the whole idea was pretty dumb, and sure not worth getting caught for, but the knife itself was something spectacular, and if he wanted to risk it, I figured I should just let him go ahead and at least try.

We picked a Saturday to pull the crime. We stepped out of the trailer late that morning, sneaking past French, who was watching TV on the sofa in his underwear with an open can of Pabst Blue Ribbon cooling in his hand. That dumb dog, Shilo, was lying right beside him, with its big head lying in French's lap. Those two were a real picture of happiness just sitting there, dazed as all hell. I followed Pill outside, watching the sun push its way west in the sky, some time close to noon maybe. We stepped through the gray gravel and the dark shadows cast by the looming mobile homes, not really saying a word to each other until we were out on the unpaved road that led into town.

"How you gonna do it?" I asked.

Pill shifted his blue stocking cap down over his scabby eyebrow. "I dunno. Stick it in my pocket, I imagine."

"How you gonna get it in your pocket?"

"I dunno."

"What happens if we get caught?" I whimpered.

"We ain't gonna get caught."

"Well, what if we do?"

"If it looks like we might get caught, I'll grab a hammer from the tool aisle and kill everybody in the store. Then we'll steal a car and drive to Texas."

That sounded like a real stupid plan, all right. I could tell even Pill wasn't so sure. He kept flipping his silver lighter open, lighting it, then slamming it closed. I had no idea where he had gotten that dandy lighter from. Stolen, for sure. I looked at him and thought once more about how nothing had really worked out for either of us since we moved. The only thing Tenderloin had given either me or my brother were feelings of recklessness and anger. We had learned we didn't have a damn thing to lose, and no matter what we were caught doing, nothing could bring us down any lower than the sad state we were already in. I guess that was where we were wrong maybe.

We walked into town that afternoon and down Main Street, where all the businesses and stores sat along the road in square buildings right beside one another. The hardware store was on the corner. It was a kind of red brick building with a green metal awning out front. There were some lawn mowers and tilling equipment sitting there beside a gumball machine. There were some big push brooms on sale, arranged beside the front door. The Saturday afternoon traffic was kind of slow. Most people must have been at the plant working overtime or at the football game at the high school or sitting at home like French with their dogs on their sofas. I watched as my brother pulled his blue stocking cap down again and stepped through the open glass door. I followed. I had never known my brother to steal anything real before, not anything expensive, I mean. Sure, we used to take candy from this store by our house back in Duluth, but that was nickel-and-dime stuff that could fit in your palm, the kind of stuff that could disappear down the front of your shirt sleeve or into your sock. Heck, both of us had taken cash out of French's wallet and my mother's purse, and even him taking Val's brassiere and that silver lighter didn't strike me as anything of real value, but this moron was going to steal a knife, a knife worth thirty-six dollars, and from right under the clerk's nose. No matter how bad either of us wanted the damn thing, I just didn't think he had the guts or the sense to do it.

I looked through the store window and saw the clerk behind the big silver register, a bald-headed man named Pete. People used to come in and say, "Morning, Pete." Then he'd nod. He didn't ever say their names back. He didn't ever say hello. All I knew was Pete sure hated me and my brother. We had been in there once before to buy mercuric acid. If you mix that stuff with some tin-foil and put it all inside a plastic soda bottle, you can make a bomb. Pill taught me that one. We used it to blow that kid Dan Goosehert's barn-shaped mailbox completely off its post. You should have seen that thing fly. *Bloom!* Then it was gone. Pieces of plastic everywhere. I guess I understood how my brother felt after he had set fire to that other kid's porch, and it wasn't good. It was like you were always one step away from being found out.

Anyway, Pill walked inside the hardware store with his hands dug deep into his pockets. He was wearing his hooded sweatshirt and some jeans. He headed down the last aisle, not making any kind of eye contact with Pete. Me, I stopped by the front to pretend to be looking at a big rack of plumbing equipment; septic tank cleaner, pipes, and hoses; I could feel Pete's stare burning through the back of my neck. I kind of squealed and turned, watching my brother circle down the aisle and walk back up to the big glass counter by the register. The store was almost completely empty. There were two big-gutted cowboys in the automotive aisle, telling each other jokes in their black-and-white snakeskin boots.

My brother edged up to the glass counter and stared down at the beautiful red knife inside. You could do anything you wanted with a knife like that. With a knife like that, you could maybe carve your name in a tree or something. You could cut something right in half. My brother's breath fogged up the glass where his nose nearly touched it. The clerk, Pete, stood over him, black eyes glaring.

"Think I can see that knife there?" Pill kind of mumbled. He held his breath, staring at Pete's steer-shaped belt buckle. "Just for a second?"

Pete finally nodded, sliding open the case door; his big white hand gripped the knife and planted it in Pill's near trembling palms. My brother's blue eyes lit up as the knife touched his skin, glowing with reflected light from the fluorescent lamps overhead. He clutched the prize tightly, flicking open its folding saw and detachable toothpick. This was the greatest knife in the world. This was the greatest knife ever. I couldn't really breathe. I stared down the first aisle, peeking around the corner, feeling my own hands trembling at my sides. This was never going to work. My brother still had no idea what he was going to do. Pete would catch us both and we would get in trouble once again. My brother tugged down his cap, still holding the knife.

"How much is it?" I could tell he was standing there thinking, wanting to just take the knife and run.

"That knife there is thirty-six dollars," Pete said. "Same as it was last week and the one before that. Hand it back now." He opened his white palm for Pill to return it. My brother kind of panicked and looked over his shoulder at me. His eyes flashed with fury and hope.

He needed to do something. He held the knife in his sweaty palm, staring down at its shiny metal blades.

"All right now, son, hand it back."

Pill looked back over his shoulder at me again. His face was all white. He was truly panicked. Pete leaned closer, his gray shadow looming across my brother's sweaty face. I kept waiting for Pill to flick the knife open and then run off, but he didn't do a thing. He just sort of sighed and handed the knife back, then slunk right out of the store. I followed, shaking my head.

"Whadya give it back for?" I asked, still kind of trembling myself.

"Shut your trap." He turned and stared back at the store.

He was just standing there, his face looking all serious. His cheeks were just beginning to get tiny black whiskers, loose and wild; he glanced out into the street, holding in his breath like he was about to cry. There was something behind his eyes that was stormy-blue and gray. They got real thin as he clenched his fists at his side. He looked me right in the face, not saying a word. He turned and faced the display of brown push brooms there on sale, nodding slowly.

I could hear that sound of the Zippo flicking open, metal against metal, and then: *Snapppppp!!!!!!!!!*

Without another word, he lit the brooms on fire. Their shiny bristles lit up like grass, sizzling and shrinking until they were all aflame, crackling orange and yellow in the silver garbage can they were standing in.

"What in the hell?!" I could hear Pete holler from inside, as the fire began eating up the broom heads and handles. My brother took off, skidding down the sidewalk and out into the street. In the only sign of camaraderie I would show, I kicked over one of the lawn mowers and started running too. He was a lot faster than me. Heck, he was older and taller. My breath hurt in my chest as I ran, trying not to let out a cry.

"Hey!" I heard someone yell from behind. "Hey you, come back here!" Maybe it was Pete from the hardware store or maybe it was someone else. I didn't know. I wasn't about to turn and look. My breath was barely coming and my belly was hurting and my lungs felt like they were on fire, and I guess I felt like bawling right there. My brother turned down an alley and grabbed me by my sweatshirt. We dodged down another alley and over a wire fence and ran toward home, covered in sweat. We didn't say a goddamn word, even when we made it to the yellow field that led back toward the trailer park. Pill stopped running, huffing hard; he hunched over and dropped his hands to his knees to breathe. His forehead was all covered in sweat and his lips were full of spit. His

face was all red. He wiped his mouth and stood up, coughing a little. His eyes were nearly running with tears.

We walked across the field, crossing down to the road; nothing settled in my mind much except how scared my older brother
had looked after he had done it, and that made me feel even
worse. He was as scared as me, all right. Maybe because he had
never lit anything like that on fire before—I mean, not somewhere
public like that, while people were just standing inside watching.
Even when he burned that kid's porch down, it was all deserted
and no one was really around. Lighting a fire right in the middle
of town in the middle of the day, that was arson, plain and simple. I looked at his face again. It was still pale and white.

"That was really great," I tried to mumble.

He didn't offer any sort of reply. He pulled his blue stocking
cap down and looked back over his shoulder to see if anyone was
coming after us. He suddenly looked a lot older to me. "Don't talk
about it now," he grunted. "Don't mention it again or I swear to
God I'll kill you."

I shrugged my shoulders and walked beside him and spit.
Nothing made any damn sense to me anymore.

And then it got a whole lot worse.

Before we reached the rows of motor homes, a white squad car
barreled down in front of us, skidding to a stop just a few feet
from where we were walking along the side of the road.

I don't think there's anything you can say that accurately
describes what you feel at a moment like that, other than doomed.
The squad car's lights were flashing, its siren screeching, the
engine hollering with steam. Pill let out a yelp and began to run
again, traversing the weeds, down into the culvert along the side
of the road, but the deputy was too quick. He hopped out of his
car, passed me, and caught hold of the back of Pill's shirt. He
knocked my brother to the ground and held him there, then

pointed to me and said: "Stay where you are, you little asshole."

My face felt all hot—I was scared as hell. I had never had a police officer swear at me before and I don't think Pill had either, not even when he lit that hedge on fire in Duluth. The police there had just sat us both down in front of our mother and French and talked about responsibility. No one—no policeman, I mean—had ever knocked my brother down and called me a little asshole before. I was pretty terrified, I guess.

I watched as my brother wrestled around in a thick pile of dirt and leaves, flailing his thin arms. He tried to kick the man in the belly, pulling himself to his feet to run again, but the deputy turned and cracked him in the nose with the back of his hand. My brother didn't utter a goddamn cry, he just held his nose and kept kicking; the two of them, my brother and the deputy, both kind of snarled and had the same dumb look in their black eyes—anger. Not just anger, but frustration, frustration that didn't have anything to do with each other or the goddamn fire at the hardware store, I suddenly thought. In that moment, it seemed to me like my brother and the deputy were exactly the same. They had both been cheated out of something they thought they had deserved maybe. They both figured they could get away with lying and cheating, but they both knew they were doomed. That's how my brother looked, lying there on his back. Already doomed.

The deputy finally slapped a pair of thick silver handcuffs on my brother's wrists and yanked him to his feet by the back of his shirt. Pill's nose began to bleed a little from one of his nostrils. He looked pathetic. The deputy pulled that beautiful silver lighter out of Pill's shirt pocket and shoved us both into the backseat of the squad car, then slammed the doors shut. He fell back into his driver's seat, coughing a little. I kind of hoped I would die just then, and I watched as the deputy turned around to face us.

"It looks like you both have a lot of explaining to do."

"Go to hell," my brother murmured, but it didn't sound brave at all, it sounded almost like a cry, like he was ready to buckle. The blood on his nose didn't help him look any tougher either. Me, I didn't say a word. I was already thinking. I thought I could blame my dumb older brother for most of it, except the part where I knocked the lawn mower over and ran, and even then I was deliberating whether my mom and this policeman might believe it was all just an accident, like maybe I hadn't known what Pill was going to do and I had maybe tripped over the lawn mower accidentally.

The deputy switched off his siren and asked us where we lived and Pill mumbled it out, and then he drove us toward the trailer park slow as hell, maybe trying to rattle us, I guess. He unrolled his window and lit up a smoke. He let the gray cloud rise from his mouth and drift up, real cool and relaxed, like he was in some movie, starring him of course. I didn't like this deputy at all. He pulled into the trailer park, right between our motor home and Mrs. Garnier's, and by then we knew he knew everything and we were done for.

He turned around in the front seat and stared at us, shaking his head.

"So you think you can just go and destroy other people's property and run off like a bunch of cowards, huh?"

We were done for, all right.

"We didn't light nothing," my brother kind of mumbled to himself. He sure was out of it. I don't know. Maybe it had nothing to do with the fire, maybe he was just so sick of being disbelieved and caught and treated like a liar and troublemaker. His eyes kind of welled up with tears and his face got all hot and red as he turned toward the car window. We had lit the can of brooms on fire, the deputy knew we had done it, but my brother couldn't let it go, he wouldn't let anyone accuse him of anything, whether it was true or not, even if they had the evidence right there in their hand. That's the real problem with lying: You never do know when you're telling the truth or not.

"I got three different folks that said you did it. And this lighter here, which all of them can identify."

"Screw off," my brother grunted.

I guess there was no hope, no hope for either of us. I thought about coming clean and spitting it all out, finally snitching on my brother, but I knew it wouldn't do any good. Maybe the deputy would think I was innocent, just a tagalong, but my mother would know the truth and punish us both for sure. I could already feel the red-hot length of French's belt against my hide. I could already hear my mother's hot crying wallowing in my ears. My lips began to tremble. I closed my eyes and opened my mouth and let it all out in one horrible flush of snot and tears.

"He did it," I choked out. "My brother did it. He said he'd kill me if I told anyone. Honest. He said he was gonna kill me if I told. Please don't tell our folks. Please. He won't ever light nothing on fire again. I swear. I swear. Please don't tell our folks."

Pill shook his head in disgust. He stared at me without saying a word, and I knew right then he hated me for sure. Maybe the whole idea of stealing something had been his to begin with, but I had gone along with him because I wanted to see him get away with it, and maybe that wasn't as bad as what he did, but I knew telling on someone was just about the lowest thing you could do. I had buckled. I had turned on my own brother. I would deserve my punishment because I was a snitch. I was a tattletale. I was a blabbermouth.

"Now ain't the time to cry, son," the deputy mumbled to me over his shoulder. "No time to cry when you go around doing stupid things like that."

He took a long drag, then opened the car door and led us out

and on up to our front porch. He knocked on the screen door just
once with a big white fist.

"Hello. Sheriff's Department!" he hollered.

French answered the door in a pair of brown pants and a dirty
T-shirt. He shook his head as he caught sight of the both of us, my
brother in handcuffs with a bloody nose and me crying like a baby;
my God, after all of my mother's warnings and French's nodding
and frowning along with her for support, they had both been right.
We were no good. We were headed straight for the pen.

The deputy flicked his cigarette out into the gray darkness
and spoke: "Looks like your boys here got themselves into some
trouble."

I watched as my mother appeared at the door, staring over
French's shoulder.

"What happened? What did you do now?" she shouted.

"We didn't do a damn thing!" Pill blurted out.

Deputy Lubbock let out a snicker. "Heh-heh, it looks like
these boys here lit a fire outside the hardware store in town. I
caught 'em with the evidence, red-handed."

"A fire?" my mother shouted. "Another fire?" She stepped
from behind French and smacked me hard on the side of my face.
That's something you don't ever want to feel, getting smacked in
the face by your own mother in front of a stranger and all.

"Pete at the hardware store said he won't press any charges,
though I tried to convince him otherwise. He said as long as these
boys don't come near the store again and they repay what they
owe, he'd be willing to let it go."

"Owe? What do ya mean, *owe?*" my brother shouted.

"Pete said it was in the neighborhood of three hundred dollars
or so."

"Three hundred dollars! We didn't even light the damn fire!"

"You best find a way to learn these boys the difference

between right and wrong, or the next time I might be forced to teach them myself. And believe me, you don't want to have to learn it from me."

Deputy Lubbock slipped his key into the silver handcuffs and turned Pill free, shoving him a little.

"We will, officer," French said with a nod, gripping Pill by his shirt.

"I want my lighter back," Pill grunted through some tears. He stared hard right into that deputy's eyes and didn't look away.

"That's official evidence now, son," the deputy said. "I'd keep any lighters or matches out of this boy's reach."

My mother and French nodded.

The deputy hopped back in his squad car and tore away, kicking up gravel and dust as he went. My mother and French shoved us inside and gave us each a whipping before we could explain anything about the knife or the deputy or the hardware store. French held me by my arm and whacked me with his belt hard on my behind without me saying another goddamn word. Then he did the same to Pill, who just stood still and didn't cry like me, gritting his teeth a little as the belt hit his behind with a thick smack. The worst part was the look on French's face: It was stern and serious, but sad and disappointed as hell. He winced with every swing, looking like he was about ready to start crying too. He held me by my shoulder afterwards and looked into my face.

"This is it, boys, this is the last fire you start, understand?"

I nodded, clearing the tears out of my eyes. Pill stayed completely still. His eyes were all hard and black and mean.

"You're both gonna end up in prison or the morgue pulling shit like that, you hear?"

I nodded again, trying to ignore my sore bottom-side. My mother was in the bathroom crying, maybe mumbling the rosary through her sobs, probably praying for both our worthless souls.

French looked at my brother sternly. "Pill, you're going to get a job to pay back what you owe."

"A job? Where am I supposed to get a job?"

"The Pig Pen. I got a fella on my line at work who knows the manager. I'll give him a call about it right now."

"I'm not working at some stupid grocery store," Pill muttered.

"Yes, you will," French replied. "And you're going to pay back every cent that you owe."

After that, French sent me and my brother to our room so fast that I still didn't have a chance to say a single word. Our damn room didn't seem any different than the prison or the morgue, I guess. Any way it went, it was like we were still both trapped. My brother laid in the top bunk, not uttering a sound, his face red as hell. I laid there too, beneath him, knowing how mad he was— not at my mother or French, or the deputy or Pete, or even the whole crummy town we both always counted on blaming—but me. Me. My brother was sore as hell at me and it had all happened before I could really think what I was trying to do or say. I had turned on my only brother and it hadn't done me any good any- way. I laid in my bed looking up, and reached out my hand to where my brother's weight made the dull blue bunk sag above. There was nothing there but the plastic skin of the old blue bed- liner. I could hear him breathing. I could hear him hating me, lying beneath his soft white sheets. I started crying again, holding my face in the pillow so he wouldn't hear. I guess maybe I tried so hard to think of something funny to say and nearly said it, but then the words were all gone and I just laid there, making sounds to myself like a prayer.

the glass eye

A couple of weeks later, it still kind of felt like the world was ending. Because I had snitched on him, my older brother refused to talk to me. I would sit next to him when was watching TV or follow him into our room and ask him how his job at the Pig Pen was, but he would just give me a dirty look and then go back to ignoring me. He was sorting through his collection of skin mags one day and I decided to maybe peruse them too, when he looked at me and said: "Don't touch any of my goddamn things." I guess he had every right to be mad. I had turned my back on him just to try to get out of trouble. And no matter how many times I tried to apologize, he just sneered and turned away, shaking his head to himself. I had hurt him worse than I had ever hurt anyone. He was my brother, my only brother, and now I had no one in that crummy town to talk to. I barely got to see him anymore, anyway. He worked nearly every day after school at the Pig Pen supermarket, trying to pay back the damage he had done to the hardware store. The rest of his checks went straight into a savings account my mother had helped him set up. He would stare at the little booklet, watching the numbers slowly adding up. And there was a pile of nudie magazines that kept growing, filling a whole shelf in Pill's dresser. My mother didn't go in our room anymore; she would stack our clean clothes outside our bedroom door. No one talked about the fire at the hardware store, neither my mom nor French. It occurred to me that if Pill had just gotten a job in the first place, he could have bought that knife instead of lighting those brooms and starting all the trouble that ended with him ignoring me. But I don't think he ever really caught on to that. He was still quietly stealing cigarettes and candy and nudie books, and then one afternoon I noticed him shove a greasy-green wad of cash into his pocket when he headed to school. After a few weeks of near silence, nothing had changed except the warnings he gave me.

"Stay away from my shit," was all he would grunt now before he walked away. That was me and my older brother.

The only other person I'd even bother talking to, Lottie, had been grounded for a month, having gotten in trouble for stealing that beautiful glass eye. During school, we would write each other notes and draw pictures of monsters no one else had ever invented—a half-tiger/half-vampire, or a Mud-Man, or a creature that was part cheetah, part lizard, part boy—but after school she wasn't allowed out of her house. By then all of the other kids in class had heard of the fire at the hardware store and no one would speak to me, let alone shoot marbles or have a spitting contest or even share a smoke.

I decided to go visit the Chief one afternoon to buy some cigarettes and bother him for some kind of company. I stepped right up to the counter with a big smile, holding some money stolen from my mother's purse in my greasy palm. I watched carefully as the Chief turned, taking a swig from his silver flask. The filling station was silent as a tomb. There was a thin gray dust coating all the candy bars near the counter and the floor looked like it hadn't been swept in weeks. There were dry insects stuck to the front windows, married to the cobwebs on the flickering lights overhead. The Chief looked bad. His eyes were deep red with fleshy gray bags. He was teetering a little in his seat, staring off into space with an empty-toothed frown.

"How are things, Chief?" I asked, not looking at him. He was staring right over my head, twitching his lips at something just out of sight.

"Fine," he grunted. The Chief's eyes turned on me then, cold and deep red.

"What is it you need?" he asked. His nose twitched a little as he cleared his throat.

"A pack of Marlboros," I said with a frown, glancing at the knot of wrinkles at the center of his forehead. The Chief dug behind the counter and placed the smokes on the white linoleum in front of me. I reached for them, but the Chief swatted my hand away and leaned over the counter close to my sweaty face.

"These things are a curse, boy. But you are too young and dumb to see that, aren't you?"

I shrugged my shoulders. I thought he was just drunk, like always, and maybe being ornery and mean. His hot breath hung in the air; he smelled like he had been pickled, like his organs had been embalmed in some kind of gasoline.

"Do you know what I think? I think I should not sell cigarettes to you anymore, boy. I think I should not add any more misery to your foolish little life."

He laughed a little, then uncapped his silver flask and spilled some more liquor into his mouth. It seemed like the only thing that made him laugh was bullshitting dumb kids like me and taking a swig from his flask. He drank deeply, then capped the lid and placed it back beneath his greasy black shirt.

"Well, what do you think? Don't you think you are already cursed?" He winked and stared at me hard.

"I don't know," I said in a mumble, looking away.

"You don't know?"

Me, I backed away and shrugged my shoulders. The stolen money felt dull and heavy in my palm, like it might slip and drop to the floor and I'd never be able to pick it up. The Chief leaned further over the counter, his face coming as close to mine as it ever had.

"It is like carrying a wound. Something that will not go away. Every day, it is always there, the curse. Every night, it is always part of you. The curse is what makes you who you are. It is what makes you who you will be. It is something you cannot escape . . . even with a good drink." He laughed, his face seeming old and wooden like the side of a maple tree. He nodded to himself once more, then leaned back. "But like I just said, you are too young and stupid to know anything."

He snickered to himself a little, then punched the register with a snarl.

"One dollar eighty-nine."

I placed the wrinkled dollars on the counter and slid them across to his gray hand. He shook his head and unfolded the bills, then hit the *Sale* button. The register opened with a ring. He slid the cigarettes across the counter without another goddamn word. His black eyes glimmered with light. Then he returned his gaze to the white space above my head, the exact spot where he had been staring before, not making a sound, not moving his eyes or nose, his lips still twitching.

Hell, I just slipped the cigarettes into my pocket and ran out of that damn place, straightening my collar as I got out onto the road. I left the damn smokes in my pocket and walked home without even lighting one, rubbing the perspiration from my forehead with my sleeve. The Chief was crazy all right. Going around scaring kids like that. I began to wonder why I bothered to go there at all. I began to wonder why the hell I even bought cigarettes in the first place.

I headed up the gravel road that led to the trailer park, then crossed between Mrs. Garnier's and Mr. Deebs's mobile homes, down one row to where Val's silver trailer stood. I had decided that I would visit her and see if we could maybe watch some TV together. But as I walked around the side of her trailer, I froze in place when I spotted a white squad car parked out front. I felt my heart go blank. Val? Not Val. I made a quick prayer that nothing awful would ever happen to her, that she would be safe. But there was the silver star that read *Sheriff* along the side of the car's door. I crept around to see what had happened, my legs shaking with each step. When I made my way around to the front of her trailer, I saw the most awful sight:

The deputy was holding Val close, kissing her softly, their lips locked together in a long embrace. A bouquet of red flowers was pressed between their bodies tight as they whispered and kept on kissing. And there were his hands on her hips. And there was her mouth moving against his lips. I felt all the spit dry on my tongue. All the blood nearly drained from my head. The sight was enough to make me sick. I picked up a stone and threw it hard against her porch and then turned around and spat into the dust. The sound of them whispering together rang loud in my ears. The quiet murmur of their lips pressed together made me want to find a mailbox of some kind to burn. I ran to our trailer and pulled open our screen door, gritting my teeth to keep from crying, hurrying toward my room.

Before I made it to the end of the hall, I saw the sorrowful stare of my mother and French, silent at our kitchen table, stopping me where I stood. They looked like a pair of parents from TV, trying to smile, sitting beside one another so quietly. French's voice spoke up, a sad little choir sealing my doom.

"Do you think we can talk to you for a minute, Dough?"

"Huh?"

French had on a long face behind his black glasses. His lips were curled in a weak smile. Him and my mother were holding hands. Her face looked like a painting of a saint. It was then that I heard the last four words I ever wanted to hear: "Your teacher called today."

"She did?"

I took a seat at the table and glanced at my mother's face. It was mostly sad-looking, not all lit up or angry. I tried to remember what I'd done in goddamn school that day. I tried to think quick so I could come up with a good lie before I walked into their trap.

"Your teacher says you haven't been doing so well with your assignments and tests and everything," my mother murmured. "She says she's afraid you might have some sort of learning disability."

"Huh?" I mumbled again. *Disability*? The word fluttered like a sickly bird around my head.

"You've been getting straight F's. You haven't passed one single test. She says all you do is draw pictures and daydream or look out the window and fall asleep. She says she's afraid you might have some sort of learning disorder."

"Huh?" It sounded like someone was trying to call me stupid, which I didn't even care to argue with. Me being not so bright was something I didn't think I could ever change.

"She says there's other things too."

"Huh? What other things?"

"She says part of the trouble isn't just your grades. She says you just don't seem to get along with any of the kids in your class. You don't talk or play with the other kids so well. And at lunch you just eat and lay your head down. She says it seems like you don't want to even try and fit in."

I didn't know what to say. My mother stared into my face, her eyes bright with silver tears. I'm sure she could see the truth without me saying another word. Of course Miss Nelson was right. Other than Lottie, I didn't have a damn friend in class or in town or in the whole world. And as far as I was concerned, the rest of those kids could burn. I didn't care if they wanted to be friends with me or not.

"Your teacher she says she wants to give you a test to see if you've got learning disabilities or not."

"A test? When?"

"Two days from now. Friday. During school."

"Friday? Why do I have to take it during class?"

"She says it'll be on all the things you oughta know. All the subjects. Even some listening skills."

My face flushed bright red. A goddamn test on Friday during school. Which meant all the kids in my class would know. I suddenly realized that Miss Nelson didn't give a damn that she was ruining my life.

"What are you thinking, pal?" French asked, still holding my mother's hand.

"Huh?" I looked up into their faces, holding back some tears. "I think I'll take that test and fail and then all of you can be glad when you finally see how dumb I really am."

"Dough!" my mother cried, biting her lips. "We just want you to be happy."

"If you wanted me to be happy, we would have never left home."

My mother hung her pretty little head low in shame.

"That's not a nice thing to say to your mother, Dough," French said, frowning. "You ought not talk to her like that."

I gritted my teeth. "Don't tell me what I can say." I didn't care how nice he treated my mother. He wasn't my father and never would be. And anyway, it was his fault, everything that happened. He was the one who forced us to move to that lousy town in the first place.

French squinted a little, making a real stern face. "We're not trying to blame you, pal. We just want what's gonna be the best for you."

"This is what I say: Nobody cared what was best before we moved to this lousy place. Now I don't have any friends and now I'm getting crummy marks. Tell me how that's supposed to be the best."

I looked over at my mother as shook her head, muffling a sob with her sleeve. French wiped his glasses off and placed them back on his nose.

"Don't think we don't see you're hurting here, Dough. But there's nothing we can do to take it all back. You yourself haven't given it much of a chance though, pal. Running around like a little maniac, stealing things and starting fires, how did you think you'd make any friends like that?"

My eyes were wet with tears now too. My hands were clenched, gripping the end of the table. French's face was a blank white plain. More than anything, I wanted to let out a growl and spit right in his goddamn eye. But something stopped me deep down in my gut. Something in me up and turned and I knew that French might somehow be right. I kicked my chair away from the table and stood, staring into his eyes.

"Tell my teacher I'll take that test and pass it just so she can see how dumb everyone else is."

French blinked and smiled a little. My mother coughed once and stopped crying, still holding French's hand. I marched into my room and laid down on my bed and buried my face in the blankets, hoping to suffocate. Tears kept rolling out of my eyes harder and harder until my mother called me for dinner, but I didn't even move. I heard French tell her to just give me some time alone. I turned over and watched my shadow on the wall until I eventually fell asleep.

When my lousy older brother came home from work, he

turned on the bedroom light since it was too much trouble to let someone suffer in goddamn peace.

"Turn off the damn light!" I shouted, and then I realized it was the first thing I had said to him in about a week. I didn't give a damn because all my lousy tears had dried and made the skin around my eyes swell and burn and it was hard to even see. I buried my head back under the pillow to go back to sleep, but I could hear my brother eating dinner by himself and French and my mother talking and watching TV and the dog howling to be taken out. When you were feeling bad, that dingy hellhole of a trailer was about the worst place to be. I gritted my teeth together to keep from shouting. I made my hands into tiny white fists at my sides and kept my eyes shut until my brother climbed in the bunk and went to sleep. I wanted to tell him that he was the worst brother a kid could ever have. I wanted to just give in and cry and tell him I didn't have a friend in the world and Val was making it with the deputy now and I had to take a goddamn test just to prove I wasn't dumb and I had made my mother cry *again* and all of us were definitely cursed, and this town, this whole town, this whole year was the worst thing that had ever happened to me— but I just kept my eyes closed and held it in to myself and stared at my hand above my face until I saw a faint cloud of breath appear against the glass of my bedroom window.

A breath upon the windowpane.

A quiet whisper in the night.

I shot up in bed, terrified, until I saw who it was. I quietly slid open the glass. Of course, it was that crazy girl, Lottie, holding her pink bike, dressed in a winter jacket and an old flannel nightgown, wearing her older brother's construction boots.

"Dough, are you still awake?"

I nearly burst out of my skin. I reached over and pulled on one of my brother's crooked blue sweatshirts and wrapped it

around me good. I climbed on down and followed Lottie around
to the back side of our trailer, where we both took seats in the dirt,
grinning like mad. My God, seeing her dirty face and one hundred
pigtails and stupid pink bike made me want to break down right
there and cry again, but I couldn't stop myself from smiling.

"Do you know what?" Lottie said quietly. "I got big news. My
older sister just had her baby. Just a couple of minutes ago."

Her face was all flushed and sweaty. It looked like she had
pedaled nonstop from her house to mine. The silver glimmer off
the trailer's siding glowed behind her hair like holy light. There
was something in her little smile that made me want to think
there was such a thing as hope. Something that made me want to
believe it all might be true. But then in a whisper that was gone
too.

"She had it right in her bed at home. But it didn't make it. It
was born blue."

"Blue?"

"It didn't even get to breathe. It was dead. Her poor baby is
dead," she mumbled.

"Dead . . . ?"

"My sister didn't get to the hospital in time so she had it right
on the bedroom floor."

Then I understood what the Chief had meant.

I was cursed. Not in a usual way, not like my old man or even
my brother, but cursed in a way to watch everyone I ever cared for
suffer around me. Cursed as my mother or French or Lottie or
even the Chief. Cursed to just stand there and watch the awful
hand of fate fall upon all the unlucky people I ever held near to
my heart. Cursed in the same way everyone else was cursed, I
guess.

"Her poor baby," Lottie whispered, her eyes wet with tiny
tears.

"Do you think your sister is all right?"

Lottie nodded. "The doctor says so anyways." Her eyes were gray and small in the dark. She nodded to herself, squeezing my arm.

"Do you know what my daddy said?" she asked in a quiet voice. He. Her father. The Devil behind the windows. The man in the dark. "He said that maybe the baby was better off to die now than to be sick and break all our hearts worse."

Lottie's eyes shimmered with more tears.

"He said that maybe it was too young to have a soul. He said if it had taken a breath and died then it would have been something, but like that it was only skin and bones."

I felt my teeth begin to chatter in my head. Maybe Lottie's old man was right. Maybe it was lucky never to breathe, never to suffer, maybe it had only been skin and bones, but it had been a part of someone else, a part of Lottie too.

"Did your sister name it?" I asked, looking away.

"No name," Lottie mumbled. "That's what the doctor put on his report. No name, no father, not even a tombstone. My dad is gonna bury it out back behind the fields without a marker to maybe help the crops grow." Her eyes became wide and dark. "Maybe that's the only reason it came. To help the plants grow."

Her face was lit like a saint and her fingers gripped my hand hard.

"I oughta go on home." Lottie frowned. "My father's probably missing me as it is."

I nodded. There was so much I wanted to tell her, so many things I think I wanted to say. But nothing seemed like it made any sense on my lips.

"Just thought you might wanna know," she said.

I saw that her eyes had run dry as she let go of my hand and hopped on her bike. She pedaled back along the dirt road, skidding from shadow to shadow up the path toward her home. I sat behind the trailer awhile longer. My fingers felt tight and stiff. I could still feel the heat of her hand upon mine.

I pulled myself back inside my window and suddenly felt like I wasn't there alone. My brother was fast asleep, snoring like a sawmill, clutching his sheets like he was in the midst of some awful dream. I shook my head and looked around. Everyone in our trailer was asleep. But there was still this feeling that someone else was in that room with me. I could feel it moving around my head, making me uneasy and uncomfortable as hell. I stared out the tiny window once more, looking for her breath.

But the glass was dry and clean.

I thought for sure that poor girl was home by now, creeping through that horrible house in the dark, trying not to make a sound, moving through the shadows and the night to find the quiet of her lonesome bed. I could see her quiet and alone, hidden under her covers. I could smell her sweet, sugary breath full of spit and fear.

I quickly pulled on my own drawers and shoes, put on my brother's stocking hat, then dug into the dark of my dresser for the cold shape of the thing I most needed, placed it in my pocket, and climbed back outside.

I felt the cold gravel as it moved right under my feet without a sound. I pulled that hat down to my eyes and crept through the dark night, walking along the culvert, but not too deep, ducking if the yellow crossbeams of a truck or car flew by. Then I was there, at the end of the lonely dirt road, hiding behind a thin barren tree. A bulb flickered in Lottie's house, right behind those blue window shades. I held in my breath, feeling the sweat spread along my back. I moved close to the ground, skipping from dark shadow to dark space, holding my body against a tree, then a woodshed that stood a few feet from her big white porch. The lightbulb flickered and I could see a form made in black, a shadow, a man's tall body as it moved behind the shade.

I stood there in the dark, fighting to breathe. The glass eye shifted against my hand, cold in the reach of my dirty coat pocket. I held it in my grasp, gritting my teeth, watching as the shadow moved and grew, pacing behind the curtain.

I knew then what I had to do. I knew why I was standing out there in Lottie's front yard in the middle of the night. I was there to save that poor girl from being frightened to death. I could feel the darkness as it loomed over me. I felt sure as hell. I never felt more scared in my life. Not scared of what was about to happen, but scared because I knew it was something I had to do. I held that glass eye tight in my palm. I felt its round shape like one single moment shared between me and her, a single moment between us made solid in time, one moment that I couldn't ignore.

I turned toward the front window and let the green glass eye go. It rolled off my fingers, a perfect throw, flying through the air without a sound, through the black space in a wide arc, until it met the glass pane of that front window and then the whole dark world broke apart. All that glass shattered and crashed with a ter-rific *BLOOM!!!* all over their porch and I was running down the road as fast as I could and I was nearly home before I could check to see that no shadows were following in the darkness of night behind me. I pulled myself into my bed and locked the window tight, curling up under the blankets of my warm blue bed, sure as hell that in a moment I would see his thin black shape and feel his hand upon my throat and then it would be just how French had said. The trap of prison or the grave.

I laid awake all night, trying to figure out a lie in case Lottie's father somehow found out it had been me. But nothing I came up with made any sense at all, so I could only hope that I hadn't been seen. I watched as the sun began to peek through the gray clouds that seemed to gather right outside me and my brother's window, trying to ask myself exactly what I had done. But there was no easy answer I could give. That glass eye now seemed like it had always been there just so I could do one thing: walk through the dark and break that front window in the middle of the night. It didn't make a damn bit of sense to me. I had no idea why I had done what I had done.

Thursday came and I stumbled through it like a fun house maze. First of all, poor Lottie wasn't even in class. I wondered all morning what had happened to her. Maybe I had dreamed the whole thing. Or maybe that glass had broken and the light finally poured in and her wicked old man had just disappeared and now she was free somehow, or maybe she had just run away. I could still feel the way her hand had cupped mine. A thing like that will stay in your heart and head for a while. It was like she was still sitting next to me all day, but when I'd look for her dumb smile, she'd just disappear. The whole school day left me feeling desperate as hell, so I decided to stop by Our Queen of Martyrs Church on the way home for some help.

I guess there was really nowhere else to turn. I was in need of a miracle, and the way I had always heard it, those things happen all the time in church. But the place was dark and empty. Of course, there was Mrs. Pheeple, the blue-haired lady who played the pipe organ at Sunday mass, humming to herself up in the balcony, paging through her sheet music for evening service, and there was an old priest I didn't recognize sitting in the very first pew, mumbling something to himself and God. There was nothing but the priest's whispers and the sighs of the organ keys being set into place, and the smell of incense and the white and blue light that cut through the stained glass windows in opaque shapes, and the clouds of dust that rose above my head from the high glass lamps and the steeple above, and the sounds of all those ghosts making their desperate prayers. I knelt in the last row and decided to do just the same.

I looked up and saw Jesus nailed up on his cross.

His hands and arms were outstretched, like he might be listening.

I closed my eyes and made up a proper prayer.

I prayed my Jesus would see that I was sincere and look into my poor heart and make a change there that would save my soul and keep me from a life filled with sadness and trouble. I knew he was the one to ask. If he could change water into wine and heal the sick and cure the blind, surely, surely the hopeless soul of an eleven-year-old couldn't be too much to ask to be saved. *Let me pass the test. Let me pass the test. Make me smart just for tomorrow. Let me pass that test.*

I opened my eyes and breathed in the dusty air.

I waited for a sound or a weird glow to appear in my heart, but there was nothing. My armpits boiled with sweat. I felt my stomach turn. Nothing changed—there was no weight lifted off my shoulders. I gripped the edge of the pew and stared up into his sad face.

No, he seemed to be saying with a frown. This was something I had to do myself. This was something I was supposed to do by myself all along. I nodded, and in my dull red heart, I understood. Jesus was right. Nothing good was ever handed out or just given away. This was something I'd have to do on my own.

I knelt in the aisle and waved at him just once with a smile.

I crossed the dirt road home and up to our front steps. Things might be okay. But it was up to me to save myself. I had to pull myself out of my own mess. I sure as hell had no idea how I was going to do a crazy stunt like that. I marched up the steps, trying to think. The screen door was open and right away I could hear my mother crying to herself somewhere inside. I stiffened a little as I saw her sitting on the floor, sobbing beside a brown cardboard box. I knew right away what was inside. All my father's put-away things. My mother looked up and forced a smile, then wiped some tears from her face, embarrassed, I guess.

"I'm sorry, baby," she said. "I don't know what gets into me. I was just cleaning and I saw the box and then I just opened it up and . . ." She bowed her head and finished off her sentence with some more crying. Then she took a deep breath and straightened herself up a little and lifted a tiny photo out of the box. "Look what I found."

I let out a sigh and stood beside her, gritting my teeth. There was nothing in that box that I wanted to look at. My old man was dead and gone. I was still feeling the curse of his life on my own. There was no photograph I cared to see that would somehow make me understand a goddamn thing about all my dark dreams. But my mother smiled, patting me on my greasy mop-head. I looked down and saw, there in her hand, a picture of me and my dad standing beside his old yellow rig. The Hornet. That's what he had called his truck. There was no faster rig on his line. The Hornet 509. He used to park that big cab out in front of our house back in Duluth and all the lousy neighborhood kids would come by and try to climb around on its huge tires and beg my old man to let them blow its horn. Sitting up in that cab on my old man's lap, wearing his cowboy hat, gripping the black wheel and tugging the horn that gave a sound like a shotgun exploding, staring out over that dashboard to the road that seemed to stretch out for millions and millions of miles, looking straight into the future and somewhere past it all, well, that was about the sweetest moment I think I ever had with him.

I gave my mom a good hug around her waist.

"It'll be okay, Mom. It'll be okay."

Once again, my mother's sweet blue eyes were sagging with tears. She placed the photograph back under some of my old man's clothes and bowed her head again. Then something in that brown box caught my eye. Something that wasn't right. I moved a pair of jeans aside and shook my head, glaring into the box without saying a word, without making a goddamn sound.

It couldn't be real. It couldn't be true.

My mother looked up with a frown. "What's the matter, baby? What's wrong?"

It was like my heart was beating full of blood. I couldn't afford a breath. I couldn't afford a whisper or sigh.

A green glass eye.

There, in the bottom of that old box, was a green glass eye.

My mother gave a little smile and lifted that thing out of its place, cupping the strange orb in the palm of her hand.

"Oh, this? This was your dad's. It used to belong to an old uncle of his. They were real close. Your daddy got it after he died."

I could hardly speak. I knew absolutely no words to say. "But . . ."

"What? What is it, babe?"

I couldn't believe it. It was like a secret being passed on from my old man. I suddenly remembered how his voice had sounded. I suddenly remembered all the lines on his face. It was impossible. It didn't make any sense. I knew I had thrown that eye through Lottie's front window. I had seen it break her glass.

"I don't think nothing makes any sense," I whispered, feeling my hands shaking at my side. I turned away a little as my mother squinted and then placed the glass eye back in the box.

"I know that's how it feels sometimes, hun. There are a lot of things I don't think I'll ever understand about your daddy dying. All we can do is try to remember him and accept what we don't get."

But I knew. I knew it was surely a sign of something.

I felt her lips kiss the side of my cheek as she turned and disappeared into the bathroom. I could hear her begin to cry all over again. The green glass eye sparkled along the bottom of the box, shining and calling and kind of speaking to me, and then, right then, right there I made a plan. I took that glass eye out of the box and made a plan to escape all the things that tied me to trouble. All my things would not end up in a cardboard box. I was not about to wind up like my old man. I ran into my room and dug under my bed for all the stolen girlie mags and cigarettes I had taken from my older brother or boosted from the gas stations and convenience stores all around town. I dumped some of them on my older brother's bed and the rest I heaved into the trash. I snapped every cigarette at its middle, then threw them all in a black plastic bag and emptied it all in the dumpster a few lots away. I stood there outside the green metal box, eyeing all my mess, staring down at the glossy mold and all the things I'd done when people like French and my mother and Jesus and my teachers told me not to. I'm sure you might say that my old man's green glass eye was only some sort of coincidence, and so everything I did that followed was some sort of mistake too, and I'd agree, but I guess I felt that a change in the heart doesn't always have to rely on the truth; more than likely it's something you just really want or need to believe. I looked down there at all the bad things I had done, smoking stolen squares and reading nudie magazines, and once again I felt like nothing had really changed at all. And so I dug down in there in the trash and saved one nudie magazine and one broken cigarette in case I had been foolish and found out all that talk about redemption and hope was just wishful thinking and I had been wrong again. I kept the magazine and the broken cigarette in my bottom drawer, with my collection of vinyl wallets from Aunt Marie and a shark's tooth and a scapular and some shotgun shells and the green glass eye from my old man.

After dinner, I read through all my books and studied as hard as I could for my goddamn exam, but French said I shouldn't worry about it, that it was not going to be that kind of test. Which was fine, because nothing I read over felt like it would settle in my head. Finally, my mother whispered me off to bed and gave me a kiss goodnight and turned off the light and shut the door and I thought about that green eye just sitting in the bottom of that drawer. I laid awake worried about how I would do on test and what it would mean for me if I didn't do so well. I wondered if my dad had been around what he might have said to me. He'd probably just say do your best and don't let anyone call you a quitter. I guess then I really began to think. I guess, lying there, I realized that all those things about my dad that I felt, all those ideas that he had been unlucky, or doomed, or worse, that my older brother and me were going to end up like him, might have been wrong. All the things that had gone bad were because of me. Me and my older brother had done what we had done and it wasn't anyone's fault but our own.

I listened to my brother's breath as he fought to sleep.

His throat sounded sore and dry. His chest sounded full of weight. I climbed out of my bed and stood beside his bunk and watched him as he slept. His face looked tired and sad. His face looked just like my dad's. In that moment, right after midnight, I was sure in my heart that both of us were going to be okay.

I could hear an animal crying somewhere in the night and I took it as some sort of sign. Right in the dark, I stood there beside his bed and folded my hands and made a prayer and mumbled it to myself until I was sure the both of us had been genuinely saved.

Tomorrow was Friday, the day of my test.

Tomorrow would come and nothing would be the same.

hell's fire has arrived

The bed above mine burned while I was asleep. I woke up and stared at a cloud of gray smoke blossoming from the top bunk. I pulled myself out of bed and watched as my older brother lit another cigarette. He was lying on his back. He was staring at a tiny spot on the ceiling somewhere above his head. His eyes looked old and tired. His one eyebrow had begun to finally grow back; a black line of hair had sprouted through the thick scab running from the base of his hair to a point right above his nose. He took a long, meaningful drag, then blew a cloud of smoke from his nose, keeping the cigarette clenched between his gray lips. He caught sight of me out of the corner of his eye and offered a smile that was grave and full of mystery.

"Go on back to sleep," he mumbled. "It ain't even dawn yet."

"I can't sleep," I whispered.

"Why's that?"

"Today's my test. I think I'm gonna fail it."

"You ain't gonna fail it. You're probably the smartest kid in that goddamn class. This whole damn town is stupid as hell."

I shook my head. "I dunno. I still think I'm gonna fail." I looked down at my bare feet. "Maybe I can just run away. Hide out in some boxcar for a while."

"You could, but it wouldn't change a thing."

"What do ya mean?"

"You can't change the way you are. You always worry about all the stupid things."

He let out some more smoke through his nose and turned on his side, staring right at me. The cigarette was clenched between his lips as his face became very stern and serious.

"If you still think there's really such things as ghosts and the Devil and curses and all of that, well, you're a goddamn fool."

He turned away and ashed his cigarette on the blue blanket beside his head. There were still a few hours left before I had to get up so I crawled back in my bed and pulled the covers up over my head and kept my eyes shut and finally fell back asleep.

When I heard the *RRRrrrrrring* of the alarm going off, I flew out of bed and made my way into the bathroom and washed my face and got dressed, and by the time I sat down to eat some breakfast, my brother was gone already. There was no cereal bowl in his place. No crumbs or spilled milk where he always sat.

"Mom, where's Pill?" I asked.

"He said he had to get to school early. Had to study for a test."

I nodded to myself and finished my cereal and glass of juice and got my things ready and stepped out the door for the worst day of life. My mother stopped me and kissed me on the top of my head.

"All you can do is your best. Now go on and make us proud, Dough," she said, and I realized this was her way of saying I was going to be all right.

I marched through the dust to school by myself, watching my lonesome shadow cross the flat gray space of the empty road. I made it to school and took my seat and just sat there dreaming of what a horror that test would be. Lottie wasn't in school again and that worried me some too. Then, before the bell rang, I heard from Mary Beth Clishim that Lottie and her sister had gone to live with their aunt in Aubrey. I didn't know what to think. I guess I felt good that they had gotten away and wished I had gone too.

After an hour or so, a woman with red hair named Miss Anne came and got me. I looked around the classroom, feeling embarrassed, then followed her, not even noticing all the nice freckles on the lady's pretty face. My whole stomach was tied in knots. We went down to the learning resource room, which I had never been to before, and Miss Anne started explaining all the different kinds of tests I would have to take, but I wasn't really listening. We got right to it then. At first, there were some puzzles and drawings, mostly shapes which I had to figure out the pattern of, those kinds of things. And then Miss Anne would say a sentence and I would have to choose a word to fill in the blank. And then she had some drawings, some of animals, even, and she would ask me to point to certain things, to see if I could follow directions, I guess. Then came the words which I did not know. I got frustrated but Miss Anne said I was doing very well, which, of course, I didn't believe.

After lunch, which I had to eat by myself down in the learning lab, there were more tests, some with more pictures, some with words, some with math. I don't think I did so well on the math. At the end of it, I closed my eyes and felt like lying my head down on my desk and just letting myself fall asleep. But I didn't. I finally noticed the freckles on Miss Anne's nose and asked her, "How did I do?"

"I think you did very well."

"Did I pass it?"

"Well, we found out some very interesting things today. You scored very high in intelligence."

"I did?"

"You did. But we just have to figure out why you're having such a hard time following directions."

"I have a hard time listening. That's what my mom says."

"Well," Miss Anne said, "I want you to know that we're going to get you some help. You'll be just fine. I don't want you to worry about it, okay?"

I didn't know what to say to that. I thanked her and she walked me back down to the classroom where I sat waiting another hour for the bell to ring. When it did, I grabbed my jacket and hurried outside. For some reason, my eyes felt hot with tears. I ran off, down to the culvert, hiding behind the tall, dry weeds. I don't know why I felt like crying, but for a little while, I kind of felt happy. Happy that the test was over and happy that the lady said I was going to be all right.

After sitting down by the irrigation pipe for a while, chasing a leopard frog, catching it, then turning it loose, I was feeling so good that I decided to walk right past my house and down the two lots to Val's silver trailer to share the good news. I was stopped still in my tracks when I saw her screen door hanging from broken hinges. There were no records playing inside. There was just the sound of the broken door swinging in the frame. I dashed up her gray steps and pressed my face to the lopsided door and whispered her name.

"Val?"

Her long white legs did not appear. There was no cloud of cigarette smoke rising from the sofa, no familiar click of her high heels against the dirty floor. But her front door was almost wide open. I peeked my head in and didn't see anybody moving inside. I glanced around at the red sofa, the Oriental screen. I looked down and saw her blue lamp broken on the floor. Two of her kitchen chairs were upturned on their sides.

"Val?" I called again.

But there was still no reply. I stepped on inside, trying not to breathe. My heart was pounding in my ears. I just knew that something terrible had happened. The broken vase and the chairs looked dead, lying there in their places. The door thrown off its

hinges swung back and forth a little with the wind. The blue
shades were drawn. I spotted one of Val's black stockings lying
alone along the middle of the floor. I spotted the other stocking a
few feet away, balled up in the hallway. "Val?" I said again, but
there was nothing. My whole heart felt empty. My hands were
kind of shaking at my side. I listened hard and heard the sound of
water dripping from her bathroom. I couldn't hold my breath any
longer. And then I saw her thin shadow moving down the hall.

"Val?" I called once more.

But her lips didn't utter a sound. I gasped as my poor Val
stepped into the light.

"Oh, Dough. Don't look at my face. Please, honey, don't look
at me right now," she whispered.

I felt my lips turn still and dry. All the blood in my veins went
cold. It couldn't be. It couldn't be.

"Please don't stare at me, baby. Don't stare at my face."

Beneath each of her eyes were two black lumps and her soft
lips had been split. There was a shiny red mark on one of her
cheeks which looked like it had been made by someone's teeth.
She was wearing a heavy black sweater and loose blue jeans. And
none of her bare skin was showing. She was hiding in the dark,
holding her hands over her face.

"What . . . what happened, Val?"

"Please, Dough."

"But what happened?"

"It was that man," she whispered. "That man came by again
last night and did this to me."

No. My teeth rattled in my head. No.

"The deputy?" I asked, clenching my fists at my side. I could
imagine his empty gray face. I could imagine his voice and all his
lies, the sight of him rearing his hand back to smack my older
brother, but now it was Val he was holding.

"Who, Mort? Of course not. Mort . . . he'd never do that. It was that man, Henry, that cowboy with . . ."

The man with the sandy-colored Stetson hat. The cowboy with the bone-handled knife.

"What happened?" I asked.

"They caught him right away. They got him last night."

"What are those?"

There by her feet were two yellow and black suitcases, old and worn. They looked packed up tight and ready to go.

"I'm going away. I'm taking a trip to visit my sister. I need to . . . get away for a little while."

"When are you coming back?"

"I don't know yet. I told Mr. Letts he could rent out the trailer until I come back."

"But what about us? What about Pill and me?"

Val came over and kissed my forehead with her bruised lips. "You'll always be with me in my heart. You'll always be with me."

"But we need you, Val. We don't want you to leave."

"I know, I know, but I have to. I have to get away now." Her dark eyes were twinkling with tears. She opened her mouth to mutter something else, but no words came out.

"But we love you . . ." I cried.

"I know. I love you too . . ." Val's face crinkled up into tears. "I . . . I'll miss you both." She covered her eyes and turned, disappearing into her bathroom.

As clear as a skull wound, there it was. Val was moving. My poor, sweet Val was already gone. I glanced around at her nice red sofa and the black screen and those lacy stockings lying there by themselves, and then I felt myself getting ill, so I ran to our trailer and straight to my room and laid down in my bed, feeling the tears I had been fighting against all day burning along my face.

"How was your test, honey?" my mother called from the kitchen.

I lifted my face from the slippery pillow and let out a cry. "I find out next week . . ."

I could hear my mother stepping down the hall toward me and my brother's room, then she was stopped by French's soft voice.

"Give the man a little time alone to just sit and think," he said. I could hear my mother place her ear against the bedroom door. I could nearly feel her lips on my cheek. I prayed to God that she wouldn't come in. After a moment or two, she walked quietly away, though I could still hear her whispering to French out there, maybe starting to cry, but then I just buried my head under my pillow, laying there, hoping I might die so I could just end all this grief once and for all.

About an hour later, though, my mother did come in. I looked up and saw the pleasant shape of her face. In the half-light, her eyes were blue and bright. I wiped the tears from my eyes and tried not to look upset.

"Dough, honey, are you okay?"

"I'm fine," I lied as best as I could.

"Val said you came by and were pretty upset."

"I said I'm fine."

She patted me on my head. "Do you want to talk about it at all?"

"No. I don't wanna talk about it ever again."

"Okay, darling. Okay. Dinner's ready if you wanna come out. French and I aren't going anywhere tonight. We'll be right out there if you want to talk, okay?"

I nodded and turned back on my side. I suddenly imagined all the lousy things that had already happened in my life: My dad dying. Us leaving our home. Moving here. Getting in trouble in school for things I never did. The Chief looking right through me. El Rey's moving away. Getting caught for starting that fire. Snitching on my brother. Lottie's old man. Her sister's baby dying. That glass eye. Taking that awful test. Having to see Val all like that.

I sat up and looked out my window and I realized the worst part of it all was how lonely I felt without my older brother, Pill, because he still wasn't really talking to me and he had always been there to help me get through it all, to tell me some dirty old joke or punch me on the arm and let me know that I wasn't alone. But now I was.

I looked out my window and stared at the night setting in. My older brother would be coming home from work soon. He'd be walking right across the road by himself, maybe whistling, smoking a cigarette, hating the way the trailer park looked, with the mobile homes stacked so tight beside one another, the exact same way I hated it seeing it every day I came home. It made me very worried suddenly, thinking about him. It made me very scared that he'd never forgive me and I'd go on being lonely forever.

I decided I had something I had to tell him. I had to tell him about Val. And how sorry I was. I wanted to say how awful I felt for ratting him out, and for some reason I just couldn't wait any longer. I had to find a way to make him want to talk to me again.

I pulled myself out of my bed and stepped into the hall, then put on my older brother's hooded sweatshirt and made for the front screen door. There was my mother and French curled up beside one another on the sofa.

"Whatcha doing there, pal?" French smiled, tapping the silver top of a beer can. I shrugged my shoulders and found the dog's brown leash.

"I'm gonna go take Shilo for a walk and wait outside for my brother to come home."

He stared at me and nodded. "That's sounds awful nice of you." He winked at me, then turned his head back around to watch the TV. My mother smiled, resting her cheek against his square shoulder.

I stepped outside, snapping the leash onto Shilo's collar. The night was cool and the sky was becoming black. I looked back through the front window and saw my mother's and French's heads resting beside one another, then I smiled to myself. Seeing the two of them like that made it seem like everything might be okay.

I walked down past the end of the lots to the field, then laid down on my back, staring up at the dark blue sky, holding that dumb dog close, watching the gray road for my brother's shadow. I knew that sooner or later it would come shrugging from out of the blackness and straight into the circles of light, and then I would apologize and he would say it was all right. I laid there a long time, running my fingers under Shilo's neck, scratching its soft white fur, searching for chiggers or fleas or ticks. Its skin was smooth and soft and nearly pink. That dog just rested beside me, breathing against my face, looking at me with its one blue-black eye. We laid there together waiting for a long time.

It was getting late as hell.

It made me worry that my older brother wasn't ever coming home.

About a half hour later, I caught sight of him, an awkward shape, grinning like a fool to himself. I crept out of the tall brown grass and met him just beside the culvert. His face was all red and glowing. He patted me on the back and just kept smiling as we walked together toward home.

"What are you smiling at?" I asked. It felt like I hadn't seen him smile in a long time.

"I don't know. I just feel like smiling."

"Did something funny happen at work?"

"You could say that." He winked at me, and almost at once I knew.

"You weren't at work, were you?"

"Nope."

"Where were you then?"

"I was with Lula Getty."

"Lula Getty? From Sunday school?"

"The one and the same."

"What were you doing?"

Pill-Bug winked at me once more. "I'll just say it's been the greatest night of my life." And then, unable to stop himself from bragging, he added, "We did it."

"You did it?"

Pill-Bug nodded.

"But how?" I asked.

"She works at the Pig Pen. A couple of weeks ago, I was out back, smoking near the loading docks, and she was there smoking too, and we just started talking, and it turns out we have a lot in common."

"Like what?"

"Like we both like wolves."

"Since when do you like wolves?"

"Since Lula Getty said she did. I took twenty bucks from my work money and went and bought her a ceramic statue of a wolf from the filling station. I gave it to her tonight."

"At work? In front of everybody?"

"No, jerk-wad. I went over to where she was babysitting. Then I gave it to her."

"Then you had sex?"

Pill nodded, winking at me again. I didn't think I had ever

seen him so happy. I was glad he was talking to me, but the closer we got to the trailer park, the worse I was beginning to feel.

Shilo hopped along by my side, rattling his metal tags like tiny chimes. There in the distance were the lights of the trailers, a glow rising over the square blocks of mobile homes. The whole place looked empty all of a sudden, now that Val was gone. I felt like everything was ending. I wanted to tell my brother what had happened, how Val had been beat up and was gone already, so that he could explain to me that somehow everything was still going to be okay, because I sure didn't feel that way. I needed him to muss up my hair or to hear him laugh. I needed to know he was still my friend.

I turned then and just blurted it all out in one gulp. "Pill, Val . . . Val . . . she's gone."

He stopped in his tracks and stared in my face. "What?"

"She left today. She's gone. Moved out."

"But what the hell for?"

"Someone beat her up. Someone broke down her goddamn screen door and tore up her whole place."

Pill went still. His face became stiff and gray. All the glow that had been in his eyes disappeared from his face. He didn't punch my arm. He didn't say a dirty joke or a goddamn word. He just turned and looked over his shoulder down the lonesome dark road.

All of a sudden, a pair of shining yellow lights appeared.

It was a swerving car, and it was coming right at us.

Headlights flashed in our eyes, as a white car with red lights on top roared to a stop right up beside us.

There he was, drunk, grinning like a lunatic behind the steering wheel.

"Hell," Pill murmured, spying over his shoulder.

I caught sight of the deputy's greasy smile, and I was almost sure that I saw him give us a cold little wink.

He slowly rolled his window down. "What you boys doing out here by yourselves tonight?" The deputy nodded to himself, leaning back in his seat.

Me, I didn't say a goddamn word. I froze in my tracks. My older brother shrugged his shoulders a little, then elbowed me to keep on walking. But I couldn't move. The lights of the trailer park now seemed so far away. And we were out here all alone. Here was that bastard's smiling white teeth. Somewhere beside his belt was his shiny silver gun. I suddenly imagined the deputy putting bullets in the both of us and kicking us down into the culvert. I swore I saw him wink again. And there was no way I could make a single move after that. Pill gave me a little shove but the deputy noticed quick.

"Stand where you are," he barked. He took out his flashlight and shined it right in our eyes, still sitting there in the driver's seat with his awful smile. "I asked you boys what it was you were doing out here tonight."

Shilo, by my side, gave a little yelp. I held its brown leash tight.

"I was just coming home from work," Pill said with a frown, gritting his teeth. He looked that bastard straight in his black eyes, then turned away.

The deputy nodded once, still grinning like mad. "And what about you, son?"

"Meeting my brother to go on home," I mumbled.

"Is that so?" The deputy shortened his smile. He let out a muffled laugh and shook his head. "Do you boys take me for some kind of goddamn fool?"

There, right there, with those words, I could feel my teeth turn to dust in my mouth. It was like seeing myself drifting toward the end of the world, then slipping closer and closer and falling right over. We were going to be in some sort of trouble again all right. The deputy's eyes were wild and bright, his lips twitching a little as he threw the damn car into park. I could hear the engine slide into neutral. Then the snap of the deputy's seat belt.

Pill just stood there, still gritting his teeth. Then all the lights around us went completely dim.

"Run!" my brother shouted, and pulled me by my sleeve. He ran straight off the side of the road and down into the culvert, towing me the whole way. Our dumb dog, Shilo, barked once then followed, hopping down the side of the road, moving quick through the wet brown grass on its three legs as fast as it could. My heart was beating right in my ears. All I could feel was my brother's hand on my sleeve, pulling me ahead, pulling straight through the dark. Our feet were moving fast, crossing over the wet grass, the dog howling along behind us.

That pair of headlights suddenly turned right on us.

"Jesus!" Pill screamed, stopping just for a second to watch the deputy drive his car off the road and down, down, down into the muddy ditch. But the damn thing didn't get stuck. It rolled slowly through the mud and straight onto the field, that pair of headlights staring right at us. "Run for the barn!" my brother shouted, still pulling on my sleeve.

Of course, it hit me hard, like a full slap to my jaw: There right ahead was the Furnham barn, standing still and red and quiet and haunted as all hell. The dog was howling and moving right in our tracks, trying to stay out of the deputy's lights. That damn barn was just ahead.

Pill stopped and turned again, fighting for breath, just as the deputy's squad car sank into a patch of dirt. Its shiny silver wheels turned and turned, throwing mud into the air. Behind the glow of the windshield, we could both see the deputy's face all hot and red and full of hate. He pounded the steering wheel with his hand about three times, then kicked open the goddamn door.

My older brother felt around in the dark for the barn door latch. Me, I held the dog right by my side, watching as that deputy's drunken form moved toward us. He was wobbling a little, losing his footing in the slippery mud, cursing to himself in grunts.

"Don't move!" the deputy hollered. "Don't make a goddamn move."

All that darkness had fallen around us. All the cold night air was coming down over our heads and I could still feel that red heat burning from behind the deputy's eyes. He stopped then and reached down and drew his sidearm. I could see it glimmer in the squad car's headlights. The gun. The gun. My heart pumped blood straight to my brain. I gripped the dog's leash tight as I could, hoping somehow that this gesture alone would keep me safe, hiding in the black shadows cast by my older brother and the barn, making all the prayers I could think of, watching as my brother swore to himself, his fingers fumbling along the barn door.

"Let me be home in bed," I kept mumbling. "Let me be home in bed."

"Stay where you are, I said!" the deputy shouted, still wobbling toward us through the dirt. Then he pointed his gun toward the sky and squeezed off a round.

BLOOOMMM!!!!!

All the blood shot from my ears and I felt myself crying, crying like a girl, mumbling more stupid prayers to myself as that man's black form kept moving close.

"Here . . ." Pill whispered. "Here!"

He slid the barn door open and shoved me inside, giving our dumb three-legged dog a push. He pulled the door closed, then yanked me by my shirt, drawing us deeper inside the dark. It was quiet and steady and full of that awful stench of death. Nothing made a sound but our breathing. Nothing moved but our shadows along the dirty wood walls. Then I made the awful mistake of stopping and looking up.

Without a doubt, I knew this place was haunted. It was darker than any nightmare I'd ever had, darker than the Devil's own shadow, covering everything with death and gloom, touching our faces like his thick burlap cloak. There were all the tiny silver spires and spindles of spiderwebs crisscrossing overhead, making all kinds of shadows which breathed and moved like a thousand tiny eyes, like a thousand tiny lips whispering my name. I could make out the shape of the sagging old horse, still lying there rotting, nesting with thousands of sleeping flies. There were the heavy wood beams creaking overhead, burned in a single spot by old man Furnham's rope. There were the old cardboard boxes of clothes and dry goods that would never be used. All these sad, sad dreams that came to die, hiding in this awful patch of wood and dirt.

My older brother tugged me toward the center of the barn, looking around for somewhere to hide, and then I could feel it, his hand was trembling, his hand against mine was cold. He was shivering like there was something here in this barn that he had seen in all his worst dreams too.

The Devil's dark red shadow swept overhead, his serpentine head shrieking with an empty smile, as the deputy fired into the night air once again.

BLOOOM!!!!!

I looked into my brother's face. He was completely quiet and still, staring up into the dark space above our heads. There it was. I could read it in his eyes. They were wide and empty and full of the same kind of fear. He had seen it too. He understood. I could feel him shaking, sweating all over, unable to keep his body still. He had seen the same thing. We had been having the same dream. Our old man had led us both here. The same stretch of lonesome road that disappeared somewhere in the dark. The same hollow shadows and blackened forms. I could almost see my old man's rig parked somewhere close. I could almost see him lying all alone, left for dead along the side of the road. I could feel the Devil moving above us in the dark, ready to strike, ready to steal both me and my brother's lives. This was it, then. The end of it all. The end of all our darkest, most hopeless dreams.

My brother pulled my shirt again and shoved me behind a stack of wooden crates. He pushed the dog beside me and then squeezed into the rest of the space, holding his breath, still gripping my arm tight.

The wide barn door creaked open.

"This is it, you little bastards! I'm warning you. Come on out now!"

The deputy squeezed off another round and then stepped inside the barn—*BLOOM!!!!!* I could feel his shadow moving right over my face. I could feel his hot breath seeping right through the air. I could feel him grinning, gripping his gun by his side tight. He might just find us and holler at us and let us go. As long as there was still some light, we might still be fine. As long as we weren't left alone with him in the dark, we could make it out okay.

The deputy grunted a little to himself, then slid the big red door closed. All the light disappeared from our faces. Immediately we fell straight back into the dark. The dog panted heavily by my side, but didn't make a sound. It held its face against my shirt and stood still between me and my brother, its thick shoulders going tense as the deputy's footsteps moved closer.

"Think this is all some game, huh, boys? All some kinda joke?"

His black shoes moved over the dirt. *Scrape. Scrape. Scrape.*

"Make a damn fool out of me, huh? Make me chase you out here in the dirt?"

His shadow wobbled a little, following his drunken steps. *Scrape. Scrape. Scrape.* Then he stopped.

"You don't know what I'm battling inside! You don't know what it is that's got me hurting!"

His voice rang like blood in his throat. I could hear him breathing hard, angry as hell, gripping that gun tight.

"All of hell's come down on me today, boys . . . Looks like you're about to get the worst end of it now."

The deputy laughed to himself a little, stopping to catch his balance. The dark space spun around him, shaking him loose. His shadow faltered, cutting across our skin.

"Where the hell am I?" he kind of whispered to himself. "Let my goddamn mind go out on me."

The dark crashed right down on his head, nearly knocking him to his knees. He staggered about a little, fighting to keep on his feet, dangling the gun by his side. All the dumb hatred and anger spun on around his skull, making him unsteady.

Then he seemed to sense something moving over his head.

Something up in the beams.

He looked up and lost his balance and fell to his knees.

"Val?" he screamed. "Val?"

He stumbled forward a little, falling against some crates. He fought for some breath, still shaking, gripping his gun in his hand tightly. He wiped some drool from his mouth and lifted his head. He fought to stand. Just stand. He squinted around to see, still buckling at his knees.

Then he caught something out of the corner of his eye.

There, right there, three shadows flashed before him in the dark. He squinted again, then nodded to himself.

"You . . ." he muttered, and cracked a smile like he was surprised, happy to have seen us there. "I found you here."

All the blood in our bodies turned cold. All our hearts turned to dust and crumbled into red dirt. My brother held my arm hard and tight. Our breath just disappeared.

"You . . ." I heard the deputy whisper. "You did this. You two little bastards . . ."

The leash went loose in my hand and all the words I had ever wanted to say my whole life poured right out of my mouth like a knife: "Kill, Shilo, kill!"

Our big white dog leapt forward and struck, clamping his jaws around the deputy's neck. Black blood flickered through the air and dotted the cold ground. My older brother had me by the sleeve of my shirt and out the goddamn barn door and into the damp gray field before we heard the cold, solitary shot ring out.

BLOOM!!!!!!

Tears fell right from out of my eyes. I knew right then we had to go back, go back in and get our poor, poor dog, to save him from all the ghosts and wicked things trapped inside, but my brother held me by my shoulders and in my awful heart I knew it was all too late, too late, too late. I fell to my knees and down into the dirt and just let myself cry. My brother held my shoulders tight as we sat like that forever, cold and still and staring at that empty barn, wishing we were all dead, me crying like mad until a siren broke through the dark, flashing with bright red lights.

The gunshots had woken all the neighbors, and within a few moments the old gray-haired sheriff arrived in his squad car, parking beside the deputy's prowler, hustling across the field in his Stetson hat and white pajama shirt.

"What happened here, boys? Where's the deputy?"

My brother just shook his head and didn't say a word and pointed to the goddamn barn.

"Okay, all right, boys, stay where you are," the sheriff huffed, and walked past us. The old gray-faced man pulled out his big shiny Smith & Wesson gun and stepped up to the barn door and listened inside. Nothing was moving. It was already done. The sheriff twitched his white mustache a little, then fought around for the barn door latch. "Goddamnit, where's the latch?!" Then he found it and gave it a pull.

The barn door opened with a creak and I stood beside my brother and looked inside and then, right then, I knew it was all over.

Our poor ol' dog was dying.

Shilo laid on its side, trembling a little in a pool of its own blood, twitching its feet and wagging its tail like the dumb dog it was. Me, I ran up past my brother and the goddamn sheriff and fell right where that poor dog laid. I ran my hand over its soft white side and saw the huge red bullet hole that had been dug in its white coat. My whole face was covered with tears but I didn't care, I didn't give a goddamn who saw me like that. That was my only dumb dog and now it was dead.

"Don't move, boy!" the sheriff shouted. "Don't move, okay?" I nodded and stayed still, holding my dog around its bloody neck, crying to myself and not caring in the least.

The sheriff stepped inside and flicked on his flashlight. The light burned through the dark and all at once the blackness separated, vanished, disappeared. But there was nothing there. There was no one in there.

"Mort?" the sheriff called out. "Mort!"

But there was no reply. Not a word or whisper. He was gone. Gone, gone from our miserable sight.

"Mort, give me a holler if you're all right! Mort?"

The sheriff stepped into the middle of the barn, shaking his head. His flashlight struck the dark red spots of the deputy's blood, which shimmered and shone, drying up in the dirt.

There was no body beside the spots. No sign of that bastard breathing his last breath.

The deputy was gone.

I lifted up my head and stared above, into the weave of cobwebs and wooden beams. It was dark up there, dark and empty
and still. The sheriff's light flashed overhead. There was nothing
there. That deputy was gone. Taken in that barn by the Devil's
horns and thick red cloak. There was nothing, not a trace, not a
shadow, not a sound, to make me believe he was still alive. In that
moment, I was certain that wherever he was now, he was worse
than dead.

"This just ain't right," the sheriff mumbled, flashing his light
into the corners of the barn. All the shadows moved and parted,
then fell back into place. But there was nothing. He had been
taken back into the darkness that had hung just over his shoulder
for most of his life. "This ain't right at all. A man just doesn't up
and disappear."

I nodded to myself, not saying a word. I held my dog around
its neck as it kept fighting to breathe, twitching its hind legs. Its
breath smelled like copper and was all warm along my sleeve.

"It's okay, boy," I whispered. "It's okay."

Our dog became still and tensed, tightening itself in my arms.
Then it was too late. Then it really was gone. I was sobbing like a
damn fool and Pill had his hand on my shoulder and the sheriff
stopped looking around and led us out of the barn and we stood
there while he searched around again.

"Mort? Mort?" we could hear the sheriff call out, but there
was no sound in reply, no sound but me and my brother breathing hard as we stared at the dark shape of that awful barn. I sat
down in the dirt and pulled my knees close to my chest and my
older brother stood right there beside me, holding my shirt, glaring hard at the outline of that barn's wooden posts cutting across
the black sky. It was done. It was all done. I could very nearly hear
what Pill was thinking, standing there, gripping my shoulder
tight—the thin snap of the match against the black strip, then the

quick burst of flame, something to burn that whole night out of his mind, something to make sure that none of this would remain in place.

He was already gone too.

That night had somehow taken all of his hope.

The sheriff stepped out of the barn and took us to his car and had the dispatcher call our folks and then they came to bring us home and me and Pill sat in the backseat of my mother's crappy blue car, unable to speak, unable to utter a goddamn word.

"What were you boys doing out there? What happened to the dog?" French asked. His face was all white like he had just seen a ghost. There were lines from a pillow along the side of his face. "What did you boys do out there?"

The lonesome road flashed under the headlights of our car as me and my brother stammered a little, trying to think of something to say. Something to explain it all. But we didn't know. We just didn't really know.

"This is it," my mother cried, turning to face us in the backseat. Her white face was serious and bare, there was no shiny blue eye shadow or lipstick. Her eyes were wide and red and sore from her tears. "This is the last time I get called on by the police. Do you understand? You're both heading off for military school in Aubrey in the spring if things don't start to change."

But I really didn't hear what she said. It was all over now and I felt like I was already home and in my bed and fast asleep and just dreaming a whole new kind of dream, a dream where you have no idea how it'll end.

Me and my brother laid in our beds, still unable to speak.

I could hear him turning over, grinding his teeth, fighting with his own awful thoughts. I laid on my back, doing the same.

What had really happened? There were things in that barn and out in the night and in my own heart that I was sure I'd never understand. Even after it all, when my poor Shilo got buried in the gray dirt beside a weeping willow right by the road, and even after someone found the Johnny Cash cassette and the goddamn bottle of sour mash in the deputy's car, even after they ruled it was some sort of awful heartbreak he sure must have felt, even after all that, there were things about that night that I just couldn't understand. Maybe that was the way. Nothing could have changed how it all ended for the deputy, I didn't think. He would have slept with someone else's wife just once and met the end of some angry husband's butcher knife before too long. I was sure of it. But my poor dog. My poor dog. There were a million ways in my head that I could have saved it. Maybe none of them would have really worked. That dumb dog wasn't born to do much more than fight and kill and then end up buried in the dirt, but it had; it had borrowed a place in my heart and marked its bloodstains on my sleeve and left a kind of quiet I did not like. But it was gone. That couldn't be changed. There was nothing for me to do but fight against all those weepy thoughts on my own.

That night I laid in my bed, hoping to hear that dumb dog's breath in my ear, but it never came. My brother was just as quiet as me, probably letting his thoughts roam outside of the trailer and onto that dark black road, past the barn and the deputy's squad car, past the whole town and fields and trees, out into the future and into some distant spot that seemed just like tomorrow but was farther and farther away still, the days that hadn't even arrived and wouldn't for some time, weeks and months and then years away, and then out into a place that finally seemed so distant that I lost track of what he might be thinking and had to just shut my eyes and give in and fall asleep.

Snappppppppp.

That night I had another dream. I dreamed my brother was sitting on the edge of my bed and was staring right at me. He

started talking to me as I was trying to sleep. He frowned a little
and patted my shoulder and whispered a quiet goodbye.

My brother was going away.

"Don't do it," I mumbled. His face looked blurry and older
than it should have been. "Don't burn it down. Don't go off and
leave."

"This is all I can do. I gotta set things right. It's gotta burn. I
need to leave. That way we'll both be free. We'll both be free."

"But it won't do any good."

"Sure it will."

"You can't just leave. What about me? And Mom? And ol'
French? What will they say?"

"They don't understand. I can't change the way I am."

"But they ain't that mad," I pleaded. "They ain't gonna really
send us away."

"No, maybe not now, pal. But it don't really matter. It's only
a matter of time before I foul up again and then that'll be it. Then
I'll be dead or in a jail or even worse. And I couldn't stand for you
to watch it all happen. Don't you worry, pal. I'll be okay. I swear.
Everything will be okay." He patted me on the shoulder like he
was so much older and disappeared into the unlit night.

That dark dream shook through my bones.

I shot out of my bed as soon as I was awake and looked up at
his empty bunk. I pulled on my jeans and shoes and ran out of the
trailer, nearly knocking the lousy screen door from its gray frame.
The sky was still blue and black, it wasn't even dawn yet, maybe
around 3 o'clock, three lonesome hours since midnight. There
were still some stars up in the sky and the clouds hadn't gathered
anywhere in view. I ran down the front steps and around the bend
of the gravel drive and then out onto the long dirt road, and right
then I could see it, sitting square against the horizon, the
Furnham's blackened barn with thick gray plumes rising from it

like ghosts, a great red fire burning brightly at the building's wooden posts.

I saw something else too, I guess.

There, like a cloud of smoke and dust, as bright as the fire but cold, a truth so cold and hollow that I could feel it in the ends of my toes.

He had been wrong. My brother had been wrong about it all.

Burning that barn wouldn't do anyone any good. Not for me or my brother or any of the memories of the things trapped inside. All those things were already done. He couldn't free himself of the past like that. Now I knew. Now I could see it. I had tried hard to bury or break all the things I didn't understand too. But seeing the fire now, I could tell it wouldn't ever work. We had both been wrong. Now he would never be free from it all. Not even by running away. Burning that building wouldn't do anyone any good. Pill could have changed. He could have made a try. But he didn't. He just lit that fire and then ran away. He hadn't learned a thing from that night. He hadn't learned a thing from living in that awful place.

The gravel was cold against my bare feet. I shut my eyes. I could feel them swelling up, ready to cry. I could almost feel that fire moving along my face. I stood there for a long time, not moving or making a noise, until I was sure that that barn had been burned completely to the ground.

The sky was still dark.

The taste of smoke hung in my throat.

The night was not yet over, but my brother was gone, long gone, never to be heard from again, left only in my mind as a name and a single shot of a photo no one had ever had the chance to take; a desperate gray-eyed boy, by himself on a silver bus, headed south, lost and alone, fighting to forget all the things that hung in his awful dreams, where the reach of a fire would somehow always glow.

Also available from Akashic Books

THE BOY DETECTIVE FAILS
by Joe Meno
*PUNK PLANET BOOKS, 328 pages, a trade paperback original, $14.95

"Atmospheric, archetypal, and surpassingly sweet, Meno's finely calibrated fantasy investigates the precincts of grief, our longing to combat chaos with reason, and the menace and magic concealed within everyday life."
—*Booklist* (starred review)

"Mood is everything here, and Meno tunes it like a master . . ."
—*Kirkus Reviews* (starred review)

"Meno's best work yet; highly recommended."
—*Library Journal* (starred review)

HAIRSTYLES OF THE DAMNED
by Joe Meno
*PUNK PLANET BOOKS, 290 pages, a trade paperback original, $13.95
a BARNES & NOBLE DISCOVER PROGRAM selection

"Captures both the sweetness and sting of adolescence with unflinching honesty."
—*Entertainment Weekly*

"It's a funny, sweet, and at times, hard-hitting story."
—*Chicago Tribune*

HOW THE HULA GIRL SINGS
by Joe Meno
212 pages, a trade paperback, $13.95

"A likable winner that should bolster Meno's reputation."
—*Publishers Weekly*

"Fans of hard-boiled pulp fiction with enjoy this novel."
—*Booklist*

PARADOXIA: A PREDATOR'S DIARY
by Lydia Lunch
with an introduction by Jerry Stahl & afterword by Thurston Moore
160 pages, a trade paperback original, $13.95

"Hubert Selby, Jr. famously said that he grew up feeling like a scream without a mouth. Lydia Lunch, one of his most celebrated—and most uncompromising—literary progeny, delivered scream, mouth, teeth, blood, hair, sperm, knife, and adrenaline in her purgatorial master-piece *Paradoxia*."
—Jerry Stahl, from the introduction

LIKE SON
by Felicia Luna Lemus
266 pages, a trade paperback original, $14.95

"With her blunt prose, Lemus doesn't waste a word in this smart, never sentimental identity novel." —*Publishers Weekly*

"A powerfully written chronicle of love, in which gender is irrelevant, and the siren call of the past threatens the present." —*Booklist*

THE GIRL WITH THE GOLDEN SHOES
by Colin Channer
with an afterword by Russell Banks
182 pages, a trade paperback, $12.95

"*The Girl with the Golden Shoes* is a nearly perfect moral fable."
—Russel Banks, from the afterword

"[A] jewel of a book. Channer's language is dancing and juicy, his humor incisive, his vision penetrating, and his hero, nicknamed Pepper for her stinging retorts, is magnificent."
—*Booklist* (starred review)